I0683304

LUNA STATION
QUARTERLY

Issue 043 | September 2020

Editor-in-Chief
Jennifer Lyn Parsons

Editors

Rocky Breen • Anna Catalano • Linda Codega
Angelica Fyfe • Shel Graves • Cathrin Hagey
Sarah McGill • Sarah Pauling • Cait Ryan
Carly Racklin • Shana Ross • Gô Shoemake
Margaret Stewart • Izzy Varju

LUNA STATION PRESS
NEW JERSEY

This collection copyright © 2020 Luna Station Press
Individual stories copyright © 2020 their respective authors

Cover illustration:
Resurrection copyright © 2020 Christina Kraus

First Paperback Edition September 2020
ISBN: 978-1-949077-18-6

All rights reserved. No part of this book may be reproduced
or transmitted in any form without the prior written
permission of the copyright holders.

Luna Station Quarterly publishes short fiction on March 1st, June 1st,
September 1st, and December 1st. For more information and submission
guidelines, please visit our website at lunastationquarterly.com

For Luna Station Press

Creative Director - Tara Quinn Lindsey
Editor-in-Chief & Founder - Jennifer Lyn Parsons

LUNA STATION PRESS

www.lunastationpress.com

CONTENTS

Editorial

Jennifer Lyn Parsons

Jennifer Lyn Parsons is a writer, programmer, and maker. With influences ranging from Laura Ingalls Wilder to Jim Jarmusch, her tales feature a rare physicality with details that feel hand-carved. When not writing code or prose, she is also the editor-in-chief of the venerable Luna Station Quarterly. She finds joy in video games, comics books, discovering music new and old, and making things out of wool, paper, and wood.

I'm fortunate enough to live with a gardener. I've been enjoying watching the plants grow, bear fruit, and now as the autumn creeps closer, I'm watching it fade. It's not a sad thing, because I know the plants will be back next year. I've been paying close attention to the way the plants have taken charge of their domain, despite the orderly rows and neat hills where they were initially planted. It reminds me a lot of how the stories I write tend to burst the bounds of the ideas I had for them originally.

That thinking led me to realize that stories are very much like gardens. Gardens come in an infinite variety of sizes, styles, and combinations of plants within their borders.

Some gardens are neat and orderly. They follow a predictable, development, maintained by the gardener so they grow sure and steady in tidy rows. However, this purposeful organization does nothing to suppress the beauty of these gardens. They can be soothing, comforting, and perhaps even contain a few surprises, if the gardener chooses to present them.

Other gardens are wild and woolly, barely contained within their beds. In these gardens, a surprise lurks around every corner and a visitor will be kept on their toes. The occasional "volunteer" plant may appear, its seeds brought in by the birds, or perhaps the wind. In these gardens, even the gardener is surprised by the result when it is in full bloom.

With both of these types of gardens, they are still only a framework for the gardener to work within. The colors and types of plants chosen ensure each garden is different from the other even if they use the same form.

Of course many gardens fall somewhere in between, with patches of predictability and wild little corners. So too is it with stories. Some carry us along familiar paths, delighting us with the little details the author inserts around hidden corners. Others are wild and adventurous, leaving us reeling with their fickle natures.

The tone, characters, and many other details of these stories are the plants of an author's garden. They can choose where to trim the hedge of the tale and where to let the edges of the story disappear beneath the vines.

The stories within this issue are each their own garden of words. The authors have tended and tilled until the tale takes on the form they envisioned. They embraced whatever twists and turns that led them to the garden you find before you.

I send you off now, to wander the paths of story our authors have created for you to explore. Go now, and seek the meadows of delight we have in store.

L S Q | 043

10 Spells the Glasbläser Family Is Not Sharing With Each Other, In Order of Secrecy

Elisabeth R Moore

Elisabeth R Moore is a short fiction writer. She and her wife live in Germany, where Moore is enrolled in a Science Communication Masters program. She writes strange stories about plants, fungi and queer women. Also, sometimes, sisters. When she's not writing, she crochets, reads, and hikes. She tweets at @willowcabins. Learn more at spacelesbian.zone

1. The spell for making lids pop off easily.

Brigit, 45

Brigit invented this spell herself. Well, she learned it from an ex-boyfriend, who told her the rough shape of the spell in an attempt to entice her to marry him. It had ginger, and acacia, and a bit of nutmeg. She had left the boyfriend, and experimented with the spell. The dried ginger powder worked, though fresh nutmeg was crucial. She kept ginger in tiny jars in the kitchen just for this reason—though only jars where the lid easily popped off.

Andreas had no idea she had a spell for this. Early in their marriage, he had complimented her jar opening skills, and asked whether or not she had a secret. In the heat of the moment, she couldn't imagine admitting that the old wives' tale of women stealing ex-boyfriend's spells was true, and so she laughed it off instead. "No magic," she'd said, flexing her muscles. "Just strength."

But the truth was, it wasn't shame that held her back from admitting the truth. Everyone was always trading "family secrets"; the free market of ideas was never really tied to blood. But she loved that Andreas had given her this—he had accepted her strength at face value, praised her in front of peers, and had never shied away from asking her for help. Birgit was better at opening jars than him, and he handed her the weird ones repeatedly. She accepted, smiled, and made sure he never saw the pinch of ginger.

2. The spell for removing food-based stains from undyed clothing.

Andreas, 44

Petra had taught him this. She'd told him so he could tell Birgit— it was one of the family spells he'd gotten during his Blessing ceremony. But the first time he'd stained his shirt over dinner, Birgit had been mad—she'd warned him it would happen twice, and even offered him her napkin. So he'd taken out that stain while it soaked in the sink, and the next morning he'd proudly shown it hadn't stuck around. He was pretty sure Birgit actually knew about this spell—she'd simply started leaving all the stained clothes in a bucket in their shared bathroom. He'd come home from work, and stub his toe on a bucket with an apron inside. He'd sigh, and grab his premixed packet (still the one his mom made him, with the ingredients written on the back in small, neat handwriting) and then start whispering the necessary words.

Yes, he was stubborn. But also: it was nice, when he came home sometimes, to be able to help Birgit, in the exact way that she needed, with no expectations that she do it herself.

3. The spell for increasing your portion size.

Petra, 74

This isn't the spell that Petra would admit to being her secret spell though—if her Gardener asked her, looked her in the eye, and waited, thread ready, Petra would tell them the spell for getting rid of herpes. No, this spell was her special secret. It was the spell for the end times. Or, a spell that helped her survive the war.

The spell required four elements—alfalfa, calamus root, fennel, and parsley. Like a few higher level spells, it was extremely picky about both freshness, and exact measurements. You couldn't pre-measure this mix—it needed to be weighed and measured and chopped moments before it was uttered.

With all that effort, she'd expected the spell to be something phenomenal when she first heard of it. But it wasn't; it didn't even double the amount of food. It increased it by about half. It couldn't be applied to a pot of stew—only to one portion of it. Outside of war times, the spell was useless. It didn't make a whole new plate, and so if you were short, it only helped if you could increase multiple people's portion sizes.

It was one of those spells that, outside of war, was forgotten. But during the war? It had been Reeder's most powerful currency. For a while there was a rumour that a child's tooth, freely given, would increase the yield of the spell. Petra had taken her youngest sister's tooth—she had consented, of course, but that was before she realised this could include pain—but it hadn't worked. She still kept the tooth in her pouch—in case.

4. The spell for reaching things that are just out of your reach.

Heike, 4

Heike learned this spell from the teenager that volunteered at the preschool. She goes three times a week, and the girl is usually there. Heike likes her, but she seems to have no interest in this work. This makes her an excellent mark.

Heike is quick and sly—she's the youngest of four after all, a classic accident child—and this girl isn't equipped to deal with her. She taught her the spell for reaching things, and even gave her a hand full of fennel seeds to complete the spell. The fennel tastes bitter in Heike's mouth, but it's definitely worth it for all the illegal things she's gotten her hands on.

5. The spell for gaining more sensation in your tongue.

Anja, 15

Anja was at that stage in her life where she experimented with magic. It was a time when you talked to all your friends, and compared strange spells, family recipes, and cultural rumors. Sometimes people explored spells, and tried to create their own.

Of course, they had all watched the very badly made presentation in school about making spells—Spells Are Tools, Not Toys—and every year for Carnival Anja's friend Ralf dressed as Dierk, The Cool Teen Who Died When He Made Spells His Toys. Yes, there was a good reason not to play with magic, but there was an even better reason to try: it was exciting. It was different. When magic worked, when Anja used a new and unusual spell—a thrill ran through her.

But really—the spells weren't the point. The point was the large bonfires out a Bombcrater Pond, the good weed, and the kissing. So really, no one would be surprised to find out that Anja's spell was a simple one—one both her grandmother and her father knew, unbeknownst to her. But right now it was her secret, one that she believed she created, and it was *phenomenal*.

6. The spell for aborting an unwanted fetus.

Catrin, 19

Catrin had one foot in the house, and one foot out. It was the problem with being the oldest child, and she knew this. She was the one to drop Heike at preschool as she went to her classes at the University. She picked up her Grandfather Torsten from his workshop, and dropped her Grandmother Petra at her sewing circles when she'd forgotten the way. She was integral to her family, and it made her all too aware that she was too young to start her own.

But she never told her mother when her monthlies stopped. She didn't even tell Martin, her boyfriend of nearly two years. She just walked straight to the Gardeners, and they gave her the spell, and a small packet of ingredients. When she bled later that day, she went to her mother, and cried in her arms. Her mother never asked about the spell—she just held her. And Catrin was so grateful.

She thought about throwing away the ingredients. But in the end, she'd felt Petra's spirit guide her, and she hid the packet under her mattress. Just in case she had to use them again.

7. The spell for sturdy walls.

Torsten, 76

Torsten kept that spell from the war. He knew there was one going around to increase portion sizes too, but he never met someone who actually knew it. Everyone seemed to know an associate who knew that one, but everyone in his social circle only knew the wall one. And there seemed to be so many recipe bags for the portion one flying around. It made it feel like it wasn't working. This one though? It worked.

His house had survived the war. Few others had.

8. The spell for having only sons.

Andreas, 44 / Jürgen, deceased

Birgit was one of four children; the three others were boys. Andreas always thought it was good luck, and then Jürgen, Birgit's father, pulled Andreas aside, and gave him the secret spell for having boys. He was amazed. He was almost positive Jürgen's wife Petra didn't know about this, and it felt wrong. Like he was manipulating something he shouldn't.

He never used it, but when they all stood around Jürgen's grave, he felt strangely guilty. He was left bearing a secret, and he didn't want it. He decided not to discuss it with his ghost though, as berating the dead was considered rude.

9. The spells for glass-blowing things. The spell for numbing your fingertips, and the spell for keeping the glass warmer for longer, and the spell for gentle pulls, and the spell for easy movements.

Torsten, 76

All these spells were combined in a song that Torsten's father had taught to him, and that Torsten was supposed to teach his only son. And yet Andreas didn't want them—he was a secondary school math teacher. He had no interest in spells around glass—he wanted spells for keeping pencils sharp and not losing his chalk. Torsten had asked him, sadly, whether or not he'd ever have any sons, so he could teach them. Andreas had shrugged, and looked away, embarrassed.

Sometimes, when Torsten watched Silke curled up in a corner, gently embroidering the trees growing in their yard, he wondered if she would ever ask him about his spells. He dearly hoped so.

10. The spell for always dividing any drink, food, or substance equally between four sisters.

Silke, 12

Silke would be happy to share this with anyone, if anyone ever asked her. No one has, as of yet.

For God is in Sleep Also, and Dreams Advise

D.L. Podlesni

D.L Podlesni writes, draws, reads, paints and occasionally teaches English in Greensboro, North Carolina. She, her husband, and her cat live in a little house close enough to the woods to hear owls, but near enough to the University that she can walk there in about 5 David Bowie tracks. Her work has appeared in Lake Effect, Writer's Digest and other literary magazines.

The papers don't always turn into history. My mother bought all the newspapers leading up to the Immigrants moving to Matewan: the discovery of the Immigrants' little planetoid hiding in the asteroid belt, NASA's reception of their distress signal, their arrival at Cape Canaveral. Nobody remembers the Immigrants anymore, though. That's nothing new in Matewan. From my high school science classroom, you could see the courthouse (since turned into a 7-11) where Smilin' Sid Hatfield was assassinated on the steps by Baldwin-Felts thugs the Company hired to put the miners in their place. For a year, Sid Hatfield was all the papers could talk about—I know, I found copies of them in a box of microfilm at the Matewan Public Library rummage sale. But you won't find him, or what happened after, in any of our state history books. No memorial, no folk tales or songs passed down. We forgot.

It's the same with the Immigrants. We forget.

I was young, younger than I realized back then, when the Immigrants started popping up at Don Blankenship High. They were green and wispy like young wheat, and quiet. It wasn't a language barrier holding their tongues, like other kinds of immigrants before them. In what more progressive Christians than the professionally dour Baptists in town called a miracle, the

Immigrants' language was similar to an older English than what Americans more civilized than us spoke. Biologists and linguists and a bunch of other ists who figure out how that kind of thing happens had their theories, but none were ever accepted wholesale. Maybe that was why the government sent them to us? Even now, we're so isolated, our English is more than a few decades behind the times. More probably nobody else wanted them, and, really, nobody else wanted us either.

The Immigrant's voices didn't quite reach a register humans should be able to hear. Collected at their lunch table under a gaudy, dime-store Rembrandt of Blankenship standing in front of the state seal, they'd talk among themselves, silent to most, the air around them vibrating with sounds too low to hear. As a stopgap measure, until the earth-air in their lungs breathed a tongue into their heads, most of the younger immigrants were taught basic sign language. With overlong fingers the wrong color, they signed with an accent.

Aside from their vibrating silence and their coloring, the Immigrants were otherwise identical to humans, a government-issue factoid our principal recited on the intercom in an unconvinced voice. Their green skin tone was akin to chlorophyll, our science teacher, Mr. Jenkins, told us, pushing his glasses up his nose with nervous excitement, while the new kids stared at the floor.

"Skin capable of generating its own energy! Bodies that hardly needed food before they drifted too far from the sun! Almost immortal!" he'd sputtered.

The arrival of aliens, actual green-from-space aliens, was beyond a blessing for a kid like me. I thought myself brave to try and befriend one, but really I was just lonesome. Lonesome and anemic and deaf enough that my demeanor and my skin tone could match theirs on my bad days. I read their rustling hands better than I understood my speaking classmates with their impossible to lip-read drawls with my dead right ear, to the delight of the girl who sat next to me in Religion.

For two weeks after she arrived, I sat silent next to her, listening with my good ear to her breathing, too nervous to speak. She looked tired, like me, but prettier. For all the government insisted the Immigrants were the same as us, as beautiful, as quiet as she was it was impossible to forget she *was* something other than human. Something better, I suspected. I felt like as awkward as a dumb boy, finding some stupid pretense to talk to her, waiting for a pencil to roll off our shared table, for one of her long green eyelashes to fall on her high cheekbone, imagining and failing a million witticisms. I was never very good at casual conversation and had not signed in years. Not since elementary, when the School for the Deaf in Bluefield lost funding. My hands were heavy with nerves as muscle memory made my fingers say :

"Hello. My name is Lydia," I finger-spelled my name first, and then showed her the sign the deaf kids had given me, an *L* brushed against both cheekbones. My name-sign indicated my most prominent feature; even as a kid, it had been the purple circles under my eyes. *"What is yours?"*

The girl's dark green lips stretched in a smile of more and better teeth than my own. She did not ask how I knew ASL but signed back.

"My name? Or the one they gave to me?"

Standard procedure had been assigning names on the Ellis Isle, the UN shuttle sent to collect her kind. Their birth names were possible, but deemed too difficult, to pronounce by humans.

She laughed, a noise like marbles rattling, a noise I could hear. A sound I could feel.

"*Stella.*" She said, finger-spelling it letter by letter. With her thin little fist she showed me an *s*, then wiggled her willow-switch fingers around her face around her face like stars sparkling. "*Stella.*"

***

When I repeat this story to my children, it will end there. Your mother was friends with one of them, and they were so beautiful and kind—that's what I'll say. The Immigrants are gone now, and how would any child born these days know to question? But as much as what happened to them was everybody's fault, it was mine too.

See, back then, I was plagued by nightmares. Not on occasion. I did not dream, I nightmared, every night. If anything came through from the other side of waking, it was a terror. It made me sleepless and strange. Of course, I wasn't the only one in town with night terrors. The world was changing. But not for us, not really, not before the Immigrants, anyway. New surgeries, new vaccines, new technologies were everywhere bringing humans closer to the immortality of the Immigrants, but not in Matewan. There was a cure for the cancers and black lung our fathers got from *still* working the mines, if the Company would pay for it. We'd all known men who were fired on obscure technicalities after management heard *the* cough. But there was still no cure for alcohol or suicide or bad romances, which was how a lot of us were killed off, or for decapitation by slate-collapse, which is how my father died. How he died every night as soon as my eyes closed. Of course, his death only gave form to a dark jumble of half remembered fears that had haunted me time out of memory. A part of me ought to have been grateful.

But grateful or not, all the nightmares stopped when I met Stella.

This! This, I thought, *this is what having a friend does.* Having a friend made nightmares stop, it made days brighter, night skies cleaner and starrier, my feet lighter, spine straighter.

Stella's signing was worse than mine, accented funny, mostly just polite phrases you learn at the early stages of any language. So we spent most of our time immersed in amiable silence, which suited both of us. We walked to school together, rope-tie walking along the disused railroad tracks. We invented signs, secret snippets of language dancing through our fingers. Like we were twins. I tied strands of fancy knots into bracelets for her skinny ankles, and she braided my hair into the snaking pattern most of the Immigrant girls wore. For a while, I think she was happy. I want to believe she was happy.

We lived near each other, as the crow flies, in almost identical houses The Company built. All the houses in town had at one time been Company houses, mine and the Immigrants' more recently so. They were cheap, but sturdy, sitting on sad little platforms of land carved out the mountain, tiered like pueblos.

I lived on top, where the best kept houses were. In the old days, the top tier was where the wealthiest people lived, mine bosses and their cronies, and their houses showed it with fresh paint and indoor plumbing. The interim tiers were what sufficed for a middle class, families who'd worked for the company for generations, all native-born Americans, who kept ivy trellises to hide their outhouses. The houses at the bottom, next to the train tracks, were the worst; where immigrants and drunks have always lived. Most houses down there to this day have uncovered wooden outhouses and only get painted (by the Chamber of Commerce, not the Company) when the Government is shopping for a new place to plunk refugees they don't want to spend much on. Before

Stella's people got there, the houses had been doused in a sickly yellow , like the color would make us forget the swirling purples and greens of the Nigerians who lived there before.

Don't misunderstand about me living on the top tier, me and mom weren't rich, even by Matewan standards. The Company had offered us renovations and controlled rent as part of dad's settlement. What were we going to do, move? I was a kid, mom was a waitress. The rest of our family was just as dead as Dad.

As far as I could tell, the Company forgot about those houses where the Immigrants lived unless the Feds paid them to remember. Stella's people weren't the first to live there and wouldn't be the last. Other immigrants—regular, from earth places—lived in them in the 1970s, when the Government sent our county checks for taking in Hmong and Vietnamese until each group found family and better job prospects elsewhere.

Stella and me walked together after school most days to my house, which had the largest lawn and most sun. If there is a God in heaven, I'm inclined to believe in his mercy or his cruelty, either one, for the weather we had when Stella first arrived. Sunnier than you ever see in Matewan, where the old folks say that the sunlight gets piped in by the Company. The same joke repeated for years like it was ever funny. The sun shone right on past what was left of the mountain and the air was humid, but light—like walking through mist around the hot springs on the other side of the mountain. Stella and me lay side by side on the grass soaking in the sunlight while it lasted.

Even so, Stella grew paler. They all did.

"A miracle of evo...God's design!" Mr Jenkins corrected himself lightning fastand pointed to Stella.

"You're adapting! You don't need to generate your own nutrition anymore, do you? You're eating food, now, right? "

Stella shrugged.

"Are you tired? You should be tired, during the transition." Mr Jenkins made a face too eager to be as sympathetic as he intended.

Stella pursed her olive lips at this suggestion. Her cast-down eyes had the look mine did when I skipped sleep to avoid my father.

"I'm sorry they're so weird to you," I told her, later, on our backs in the grass of my yard. "They get like this about all refugees, not just ya'll. Shoulda seen when the Sudanese were here—least ya'll don't have an accent to make fun of." She could hear just fine, all of them could, just not speak.

Not a problem, she rumbled back. Lying close like that, I could feel the vibrations if she tried to speak, well enough that she could say simple things and I would understand.

"I'll say something to them. Ain't like you're a circus freak or nothin'."

That time I just felt her head shake "no" halfhearted, and she rested her forehead against mine. Her skin was so cool. As I had gotten closer to her, as her green faded, it became easier to forget she was something different than me, not human. She was my friend, I thought, more important than her species.

Her skin was so cool. Almost cold.

You know how the news reports said the whole thing came as a shock? That's a damn lie. An immigrant who I didn't know, identical to Stella, only broader and with shorter hair, killed himself the first week of October, right when it started to get cold. Another pair followed. Those suicides, in and of themselves, were nothing to be alarmed about; suicide is catching, and death comes in threes. Least that's what the old folks say, and they lived to get old somehow. I figure they'd know.

Same thing happens to us every five years or so, killing spells come and pass and we aren't too much worse for it. But those Immigrant kids...they must have *researched* how to die. How else would they know? Centuries...the Immigrants were supposed to live on their own planet. The paper didn't release how they had done it, maybe trying to prevent what ended up happening anyway. I asked Stella if I could go with her to the funerals, and she had just laughed. Leaning against me, so I could feel the vibrations of her speech, she rumbled: "So kind. But we have no funerals. Why would we?"

For her part, Stella was as stoic as ever. I had at first believed her silence was due to her grade-school signing vocabulary. Late in the year, it was too cold to lay in the ever-dwindling sunlight. Young and greedy and foolish like I was, I didn't notice the change in the timbre of her silence. I felt so good! I had never, not ever in my life slept so well. When I slept I dreamt of Stella, of her humming on the ground next to me, of us signing under the table in science class. I slept the sleep of the young, I dreamt the dreams of lovers.

"How do you live here?" Stella asked me, her hands making the signs small, as if her fingers were whispering, as we laid on the browning grass outside my mother's house. The ground under us was cold and sunsets were coming earlier and earlier, but we had a few good weeks until winter. Matewan had not shown Stella our best face. There had not even been an offer of a memorial for the kids who killed themselves, no real attempt to assimilate the few Immigrant adults. Even the Methodists hadn't tried to woo the Immigrants with muffins and invitations to hayrides when

they first arrived, as was their custom with every previous immigrant group. The Baptists had gone so far as to post "Jesus loves all the children of the WORLD" on their placard out front. The world. *Our* world.

If memory serves, as it only sometimes does, that day had been rough on Stella in particular. Sister Agnes, the "bible literature" teacher, had lit into one of her infamous lessons on Hell. The lecture, and the cranked-up thermostat accompanying, it was the stuff of Don Blankenship High legend. It was a blessing for Agnes that our civics instruction had been as slipshod as it was. None of us thought to question the legality of sermons disguised as lectures in a "literature" class, much less thought to do anything about it.

Sister Agnes raged harder that year, in the presence of beings she deemed even further outside God's graces than human non-Catholics like me.

"Sister Agnes?" I asked Stella, with my hands and my voice. I was teaching her new signs until her voice grew in. "Don't worry about her. She's a bitch."

Stella shook her head, her hands, nearly white, and now said: *"When you sleep, how can you live like this?"*

"What do you mean?"

"Every night..." She looked up into the sky, away from me. Her hair, once the pearly color of cornsilk, had browned at the tips and blended into the dying grass. She lay her head next to mine, so I could feel her rumbling as clear as if she'd spoken: *"I see these things...awful things. While I sleep. Every night."*

"Nightmares. They happen to everybody. Didn't they happen... back home?" I asked, avoiding naming her old planet, by then a barren rock hanging in space, where those who had not been lucky enough to fit on the UN shuttle to Earth waited in darkness to die.

Stella shook her head.

I put a cautious hand to her shoulder, a gesture I'd seen other girls make toward each other but never had occasion to make myself.

"*A man. His head...*" Stella drew a finger across her neck, not knowing the word. I felt sick. "*He looks like you.*"

I had never told her about my father. It was possible she knew; as common as mining deaths were, Dad's was gruesome enough to be famous. I should have known. Who else did she talk to but me? How else would she have seen?

"They're just part of being human," I told her instead. Not like I was lying. Nightmares were in our genes. They were directive. Malignant, terrible things who had their place. "*God is in sleep also, and dreams advise*" Dad always quoted to me when I woke him up with one of my terrors, before he turned into them. I never learned who taught him the line—he was not the literary type.

"*I'm not human,*" Stella rumbled back.

"It's catching, Stel," I smiled.

She raised a hand to speak, but dropped it, the weight against the ground like a bird dropping from flight. She turned, pressing her forehead against mine. We laid in silence until the last smattering of light faded into black. Stella walked home alone. I watched her disappear into the darkness down the hill. I hadn't offered to walk her home.

It was cold. I was selfish.

That night I slept deep, like a stone dropped in still water. That night I had the last nightmare of my life, perhaps the last nightmare of our generation. Dreams are boring to hear about and bad luck to tell them if a listener has already eaten. I will take the risk, as I will never tell this story again. In the stillness of sleep, I nightmared:

We are sitting in Religion class, me and Stella, and she's dozed off. Her elbow on the table, holding her head in one hand, and every time she falls too deep asleep, she sways forward and wakes up. Every time she wakes her eyes go wide, wider, wider, until her face is all eyes. All thick eyelashes and swooping brow, all purple-tinged green circles, like the unfolded leaves of a prayer plant. The proportions seem off, I think in dream logic, and I realize I *am* asleep and in my own head, in my own bed, and the things around me are only as real as I allow. The classroom around us changes into different places, as places in dreams are wont to do. Blink: the brown grass of my mother's lawn. Blink: Mr. Jenkin's science class. Blink: orange-red evening balancing on the railroad ties. Blink: Dark, cold, the distant glimmer of Earth just visible from Stella's barren homeland. It's hot, like Sister Agnes had set fire to the room to drive her point home.

Suddenly, there is a scream—a deep, sternum-rattling scream next to me, and it is Stella, pulling at her hair, fallen out of her chair. I look around and know I am the only one who can hear her, that her voice resonates in my bad ear, the one dead one. In a voice lower than anyone else's healthy ears can hear she hollers, "These aren't even mine! They aren't even mine!" I drop to her side, try to hold her as scenes flicker around us. No one notices either of us, even as her sub-sonic screams rattle the windows. A great tongue of flame wraps around the room, and I watch it eat up every nightmare I've ever had. The whole room on fire, Stella

33

and me are all that's left, and I pull her close to me, shout in a voice like hers, but she can't hear for her own screaming.

***

Back home, in the waking world, a siren from the bottom of the mountain blinked my eyes open, and I laid there trying to cry out for what felt like a very long time before my throat crackled, allowing a broken yelp. Yes, Dad, God is in sleep, dreams advise, but there's a good science for this, reason enough: I was not a stranger to sleep paralysis, to the horrifying trapped-in-my-own-skin regaining consciousness. The end of sleep where dreaming happens is susceptible to outside influence, and the sirens were so close, so even as deaf as I am, they made it through to my subconscious without managing to rouse the parts of my brain that made me move or scream.

Walking out to the porch in my bare feet, I should have known what I would find. That's the part that was my fault. I was Stella's friend, I knew, in my bones. I should have helped. I should have walked her home. I should have asked...I have so many should-haves about Stella, about the Immigrants, about everybody. I will spend the rest of my life listing should-haves. I will stand before the throne of Judgement with a mouth full of "should-haves" stacked down my throat. Standing on the porch in my bare feet, I should have known what I would find.

The bottom of the mountain was a row of flame. The ramshackle houses by the train tracks lit the early morning sky orange, the air itself glowing with fire. The smell was like burning young, green wood.

As human as they appeared by the end, the Immigrants were not the same as us. They couldn't bleed, couldn't starve, aged only so much, wouldn't smother; without direct intervention, they were almost immortal. Almost.

On the news in the next few weeks, different county officials tried to explain what happened. Said we weren't planetist. We had no idea the Immigrants were suffering so much that immolating themselves was preferable to another day in our town, on our planet. We'd been so welcoming, they said, we'd tried so hard, but the Immigrants kept to themselves. In a few weeks, stories started seeping in of other Immigrant settlements elsewhere disappearing in the same way.

"A senseless tragedy." A newswoman said, standing in front of the burned-out Company houses, desolate as the planetoid the Immigrants had abandoned. I expected that night to meet Stella aflame in sleep, for her to join my father. Only after a week of quiet sleep, alone in my head, did I piece together what had happened.

Our nightmares abandoned us. Parasites, nightmares would have more time to live on the almost-immortal Immigrants, innocents with no defense against them. It wasn't fair. Stories that didn't belong to them, incomprehensible terrors not of their world shattered the Immigrants. Our nightmares wouldn't suffer such beautiful things as the Immigrants to live uninfected by the dread lived and breathed.

I haven't had a nightmare or even heard of someone having one in years. My younger self would think me insane for missing nightmares, but in the hours before my colorless, meaningless sleep overtakes me these days, I do. In those hours I believe Dad, and whoever read Milton to him, was right: without my dreams, I am sleepwalking through life, unadvised. God himself was lit up in that pillar of flame by the train tracks. Miracles made flesh were delivered to our doorsteps and we ignored them, turned them away, were suspicious of them.

I am alone all over again. My memories of Dad and Stella are just flat images my waking mind can manipulate at will. For the most part, I have given up on sleep. Most nights, I sit on my mother's porch and look down the mountain, where Stella used to live.

The County never rebuilt the houses. There was some dispute between the County and the Company over who owned them in the first place, and by the time the Company's lawyers had sorted the whole thing out it was too late. Quicker than kudzu and stronger than diamonds, a strange new knot of trees appeared by the train tracks, a tangled forest of silver wood and willowy leaves. No one knows what to make of it. The Government even sent in botanists from DC to collect samples, but the trees' shining bark would not yield and they left empty-handed.

On nights when rest seems pointless, I walk down there to stroke the smoothness of their twisting trunks, to hear the buzz that nobody else will admit to hearing—if they can hear it at all.

"Stella?" I call into the night.

The trees hum with my heartbeat, and I know they'll be back— my nightmares, the Immigrants, all of them. I used to ask myself, "Did I need my nightmares, to be human?"

An inane question, one a child could answer.

In the starlit shade of that overnight forest, my question is different now.

What will we be when they come back?

Yolk

Morgan MacVaugh

Morgan MacVaugh is a home-grown
writer from Lancaster, PA. She likes
card games, oil paints, and her chonky
black cat. You can find some of her
other work in CrabFat Magazine,
Gingerbread House, and F(r)iction's
Dually Noted series.

There was once a very lonely man—or the closest thing to a man that was not quite one—who spent his time in the sliver of light exactly between night and day. He dipped his fingertips in the yolk of new-day suns, and felt against his cheeks the electricity of stars crackling past. He walked the globe's circle again and again just to stay in that precious band of teal and turquoise that he had grown comforted between.

He walked constantly. His calves were carved meteor and his steps looked like jet lines to any person who happened to glance up at the sunset-or-rise for a brief moment in their busy days. But he knew nothing of the people down on earth.

He knew nothing human or earthly, save for the birds flying south in the fall, and their kin that returned in the spring. Though he did admit to himself once softly, during a particularly dark and long eclipse, that the birds did not choose to fly for him. Their nature was the same as his, to journey and return in the same path that they had etched into the air at the beginning of time. Then retracing, retracing. The man felt that they were one and the same, but he was still alone. The thought had been so alarming that he danced and wriggled his limbs, jiggling it quite out and away.

And so he grew to not care particularly for the birds, or the fall or the spring, or about the funny little cookie-cutter people running about beneath him on the earth.

He knew no one.

That isn't to say, however, that no knew him.

***

One person—a not-quite-child-not-quite-grown person—discovered him the day of the eclipse. She remembered it well, not simply for the eclipse, but because that was the day she had cut down the family clothesline with her father's heavy, rusted gardening shears. (The string, she reasoned, would be much better suited to hoisting the sails on the miniature sailboat she was christening later down at the pond.) She had jump-roped down to the water's edge with her mother's yells echoing behind her.

It was then that the black water grew blacker and the green fields around her dimmed and she feared the wrath of her mother had actually caused the world to stop this time. But she looked up at the sun melting away and saw him, still and alone and lost-looking when the whole world was going dark.

After the eclipse, she didn't stop looking. She always found him walking across the first or last strip of horizon light.

Then she spent some time growing, getting dirt under her nails and eating the bright tomatoes from her father's garden as juice dribbled down her chin. She grew, sowing rows of seeds into the churned-up ground with her father, and sipping on her mother's honey tea in the winter. Every evening of every year was spent like that, sitting with each other and breathing in the others' laughter.

As for the man, she couldn't say what he did after he walked stiltedly against the skyline and disappeared again on the other side. She hoped he sat down to rest with someone he cared about as night fell. But as the days turned into months and the months to years, she got the sneaking suspicion that every night he walked the globe straight through 'til dawn on the other side of the world, then again and again and again.

Through the band of light she saw loneliness pretty clearly. So one day she slipped on some old sneakers and a knit cap her mother had made the previous winter (to catch the parts of her that were in danger of flying away). She cut and wrapped a few thick slices of bread from the morning's loaf and shoveled the family toaster into her fraying satchel. She met her mom at the door as she left, and informed her she might be back tonight, tomorrow, or a year from now. Her mother fondly rolled her eyes and wished her luck.

Then she stepped out through the garden to the little rusting gate at the entrance of their home. Her father was wiping sweat off his brow and leaning over heads of lettuce with a spade. She smiled and told him she'd only be a minute.

***

The girl walked longer and farther than she ever thought possible, to get to the place where the sky touched the earth. It took a great deal longer than she thought, as her house and then her town melted into doll house sizes and the pine grew thick around her. The incline, of course, was the worst of it. Naturally it came at the end.

She made it to the highest point that she could climb with just enough time to catch her breath and sit a moment. The daylight ebbed and softened around her. The pines cooled. The glow of the world gave way to sunset and twilight, and she saw the man walking above her.

She stood up and called out to him, just some soul noise that broke free through her lips. (It was a lot of whooping and hollering, very wolflike in the mind of the girl but very human to the wolves far off in the pines.) Maybe it was his name, or maybe not, but the point is that he looked. So she gave up noise-making and waved ferociously with her entire arm as means of introduction. He could only stare. The stars began to set lower and hang above his head. She motioned to them frantically and clasped her hands together.

Now the man had not quite quit his walking during this exchange. (It was not in his manner, especially as he was unsettled and surprised and unsure of this little cookie-cutter person suddenly howling on his doorstep.) But just when he felt his heart might patter away without him, he reached for the stars hovering above and grasped one that was barely bigger than his palm. He tossed it down to the girl as he left with the light, disappearing behind pine and mountain. He only just saw her catch it as the world went dark behind him.

***

The girl expected the star to scorch her hands, or catch fire to her clothes, but it didn't hurt at all. So she wiped her eyes with the back of her sleeve and thanked the star for keeping her company through the night, along with the trees and the fireflies and the soft breeze that was coming down over the hill and smelling like autumn. She thanked everything she saw until it was properly dark and she couldn't see anything anymore. Then, she dared not sleep for fear it was all a dream, so she hugged the star to her chest and whispered the stories and songs her mother had taught her eons ago. This went on until the first grey hum of morning started over the mountain.

***

Quick as she could, she set the star down and dumped her satchel at her feet. The toaster settled its legs into the undergrowth as the girl got the bread unwrapped and slid into the slots. She lifted and plugged the cord into the little star (who had okayed it in the night with their conversing) and the toaster fizzled and jumped, its heat coils burning like flames in the hearth back home.

The toast was done just as they grey of morning grew into teal. The girl picked up the star and tossed her toast into the satchel around her shoulders. Along the left of the mountain line, the man came walking.

She whistled and waved. The man, this time, was surprised enough to stop to stare at the person who hadn't gone away in the night. She tossed the star up at him (with a whispered goodbye) and he just barely caught it. Her hand stretched towards him. The star jumped from his palm, floating back to its fading kin far above the band of light. Kneeling, the man grasped the girl's hand and lifted her up just as the first soupy bead of light crested over the mountain.

The toast was semi-squished in her satchel, but it didn't seem to matter as the girl handed the man a slice and picked one of her own. The orange, orange sun bubbled beneath their perch, beneath that shelf of teal and turquoise exactly between night and day. Their legs dangled as they dipped their toast into the sun's molten yolk and it tasted so good. Like gardens in bloom and starlight in summer and trees and mountains and not-quite-men and not-quite-women and not-even-close-to-cookie-cut-people. They dipped and ate and laughed until the yolk dribbled out of their mouths and onto the girl's jeans and man's carved legs, leaving singe marks.

***

The moment couldn't have lasted much more than a few minutes or hours—whichever was shorter—before he helped her touch the earth again and she helped him smile even as they both parted and waved.

For the waving wasn't the kind that said goodbye. Not really. It was the kind that said, *See you soon.* Or, *I had so much fun.* Or, *I will always have this in my mind and be looking for a chance to have it again.* 'Cause it was easy, too easy, they both found—as the man caught the urge to look for the birds, and the girl skipped back down the mountain dreaming of home—to look up or down or behind when everything was altogether too much and too little. Looking forward was harder.

Though perhaps less so, when there was at least something, or someone, waiting ahead. Maybe with a toaster.

A Worship

Andrea Goyan

Andrea is a writer, actress, painter, and Master Pilates Teacher. Recent stories can be found in The Dark Sire, 101 Words, Sirens Call Publications (issue 48), Halloween Party 2019, On Loss: An Anthology, Dirty Girls Magazine (May 2019), and Newfound Journal (October 2018). She's an accomplished playwright. Her monologue "Goodbye" appeared in the Lockdown Monologue Festival 2020 at www.suki.tv. Many of her plays have been produced in Los Angeles where she lives with her husband, a dog, and two cats.More at Facebook: Andrea Goyan Storyteller, andreagoyan.com, Instagram: @andreagoyan

Detective Angie Ferguson wasn't sure what she was looking at. The dead man's skin appeared to hug his bones, taut as a mummy's wrapping. As she pressed a gloved finger against his arm, it was met with dried flesh the consistency of jerky. Nothing soft or fluid remained in the body. If she'd had to guess, she'd say the man had been dead for years. But he hadn't. The deceased was one Henry Van Patten, missing less than twenty-four hours. His wife reported him missing after he didn't come home for dinner the previous evening. Henry had spent the day harvesting their Brussels sprouts crop. It was hard work, bending down, twisting the sprouts until they'd snapped off the stalk; it made a man hungry. So, his wife had prepared a hearty meal to match his appetite. She left it out on the table until the meat grew cold and the cheese on top of the macaroni hard. At that point, Mrs. Van Patten put everything into Tupperware containers to store in the refrigerator.

Then she called the police.

At daybreak, his field hand found the body, supine. His torso, arms, and upper legs were partially supported by the sturdy stalks, so only his feet touched the ground. Angie held a hand over her eyes to block the sun as she looked out over the farm. The stalks might've been pretty earlier in the year, but now all she saw was row upon row of dark-green butt-ugly plants. Dirt below, harsh sun above, a massive irrigation system—a bee landed on her arm—and insects. Angie blew on the bee and it whirred past her head as it flew away. Farmers' lives were anything but glamorous.

While the coroner secured the body, Angie pulled off her gloves and scrolled through the missing person report on her phone. Nothing in the account, detailed by an Officer Benton, appeared abnormal. Benton went to the residence the previous evening to take Mrs. Van Patten's statement, and found "the missus pacing on the porch wringing her hands." The officer logged the finished document into the system upon completing his interview at 2030 hours. Angie flashed back to where she'd been at 2030, a local dive bar catching a buzz. Two beers and a shot of whiskey. Nightcap for an uneasy mind. These days, she wasn't sure if her hyperactive mind led her to her career or if her career made it difficult to turn off her brain. It didn't really matter; it was a chicken egg riddle. Besides, her habits weren't in question here. She needed to find out what happened to Henry Van Patten while his wife worried the floorboards.

She glanced over to see the coroner zip the body bag then return to reading the report.

The officer's line of questioning had continued in an orderly fashion.

"When did you last see your husband?" he'd asked.

"Lunchtime," Mrs. Van Patten told him. "Henry never misses a meal."

Which meant, Angie surmised, he was already dead by the time Officer Benton arrived at their home. Poor Mrs. Van Patten hadn't known she was a widow when she'd called the police. In her mind, she was still the wife of Van Patten. Angie lingered; woman, wife, widow, why did all those nouns to describe females begin with double-ues? Coincidence? Probably, but those types of details plagued Angie. They were the minutiae that made her a good detective and also the things that kept her awake on nights when she should've been sleeping. She read on.

"Maybe something he ate disagreed with him?" Officer Benton asked.

That question wasn't protocol, but Angie knew he'd been assessing whether the farmer's wife/widow was guilty of any foul play. And though Angie hadn't been present, she knew by the woman's answer, that Mrs. Van Patten hadn't liked the question one little bit.

"He ate the same thing he eats every day this time of year. Crop's good. We eat off our farm."

She'd probably scrunched her face into an unforgiving grimace, an expression Angie was all too familiar with. One thing she'd learned living in a farm community: don't make disparaging remarks about anyone's home cooking. Or, their land.

The officer then asked whether Mr. Van Patten had any enemies.

"For crying out loud," Mrs. Van Patten said. "My husband's a farmer. His only enemies are the soil the Good Lord gave us and the weather He sees fit to deliver. Piece of hell this land. Amazing Henry's ever been able to get a crop off of it."

Women like this farmer's wife/widow peopled almost every farmhouse Angie had ever entered. Hard-working, no-nonsense women. Women who didn't show their hands to strangers, who seldom smiled, and who certainly didn't reveal any humor they'd secreted up their sleeves. And now, Angie would notify her of her husband's death, reinforcing for Mrs. Van Patten that life was the godawful fight she'd always believed it to be.

Angie pocketed her phone and approached the coroner as he loaded the corpse into his van.

"What do you make of it?" she asked.

The coroner shrugged. "Strangest thing I've ever seen."

"Yep."

The coroner climbed into the van. "I want to show you something."

Angie clambered up, her five-foot frame making it a more significant struggle than she wanted to admit. But once inside, she could stand straight, while the coroner needed to crouch down to avoid hitting the roof. Angie was relieved to get out of the sun. A dull throb in her temple reminded her she'd missed her morning coffee in her hurry to get to the farm, and standing in the sun exacerbated the pain. A double-whammy. On her way to see the widow, she'd grab some water and caffeine and bounce right back.

"What do you want me to see?" she asked.

The body lay on the gurney between them, she watched as the coroner slipped on a new pair of gloves before opening the bag. Even in the dim light, Angie remained struck by the oddness of the body.

"Almost doesn't look human," she said in a hushed voice.

"Watch this," the coroner said, placing a hand against the corpse's neck.

"I'm looking at...?"

"Not looking...listening."

The gloves stuck for a moment as he pulled his hand away, sounding a bit like a Band-Aid being ripped off someone's skin.

"What the...? He's sticky?" Angie said.

The coroner nodded. "I noticed that when I got him into the bag. His body is covered in something like honey."

Angie shivered. She loved honey. Now she knew she'd never be able to eat it again. The vision of this sticky corpse would flash before her any time honey was mentioned. Hell, everything about these remains would be indelibly inked in her memory forever. One of the hazards of the job and of her exquisite ability to recollect facts. Grabbing onto the side of the van's door, she hopped back down to the ground.

"Let me know what you find. I'm heading out to the widow."

He nodded and rezipped the bag. "I hope to have some kind of preliminary by end of day."

***

Mrs. Van Patten sat on her porch swing staring straight ahead, as Angie pulled her car in front of the white clapboard farmhouse. Even when Angie slammed her front door, the woman gave no notice to her.

Gravel crunched beneath Angie's feet. "Ma'am," she said, stepping onto the first step.

"I told him not to buy this land," the woman said. "When he first brought me to see it. I said, 'Henry, it'll be the death of you.'"

Angie stopped advancing, her hand resting on the wooden railing. One of her fingers picked at a fleck of loose paint. "How'd you figure?" she asked.

Mrs. Van Patten turned to look at the detective.

"My father was a farmer, corn mostly. Farming's all I know. This land wasn't meant for crops. Soil's not rich enough. But Henry wouldn't hear it. Said all she needed was his TLC." She looked away from Angie and kicked against the porch planks with all her might, sending the swing careening. It wobbled, teetering to and fro beneath her ample girth. "He never should've listened to city folk about things they don't know nothing about." The rubber soles of her shoes squealed as she planted her feet down hard. The swing came to a stop. Mrs. Van Patten turned to face Angie again. "And now there's a funeral to plan."

Angie nodded, noting that this was the moment when Mrs. Van Patten officially changed from wife to widow, and Henry Van Patten's life changed from present to past.

Anger was nothing new in Angie's world. Those left behind were always angry. At their loved ones, at God, at the person responsible for their death, at themselves, hell sometimes at the food in the refrigerator (though never anything they'd already prepared). Angie had stopped taking it personally years ago around the time she realized she wasn't their mother, or lover, or priest. Her job was to help them figure out where and on whom they should focus all their rage. Now she would do that for the widow Van Patten.

Angie slipped back into her driver's seat and took a swig of lukewarm coffee. It was time for her to check in with Lou Fines, the field hand who'd found the body.

Mr. Fines lived in a one-room house in one of the region's informal migrant camps. The house was freshly painted. Pots of tomatoes and basil and some other plants Angie pretended not to recognize surrounded it. She knocked, and a man in his mid-fifties opened the door. At least she guessed he was in his fifties, his weather-worn face might've aged him ten or twenty years. Angie tried to take those things into consideration, and though his age didn't matter in this case, guessing it was a game she liked to play.

"This about Henry?" he said.

"Yes," Angie said, flashing her badge.

He glanced down to where his seedling marijuana plants grew.

Angie smiled. "Too late to hide them, Mr. Fines. But at this point in their growth, I figure they could be just about any sprout. Except Brussels."

Fines slipped outside, closing his door behind him.

"Got a cat. Coyotes kill it if he gets out."

He gestured to one of the two wooden dining chairs set out on the porch facing the dirt road where she'd parked. They each took a seat. An ashtray filled with soot and roaches sat on the small metal table sandwiched between them. A dog barked in the distance. For a moment they appeared like two friends ruminating over the weather or the price of corn in a deflated economy.

Fines cleared his throat. "How can I help you?"

Angie leaned forward. Her chair wobbled.

Fines shook his head. "One day, I'll get around to fixing that thing."

"Can you tell me about Henry?"

"That's not what I thought you'd ask."

"His widow says he didn't know what he was doing."

Fines took off his cap and rubbed the top of his balding head. "Excuse me, but his wife's a piece of work." He slipped his cap back on.

Angie laughed, then said, "Yes. She does seem opinionated."

"Look, I'm not a young man, but I'm willing to change with the times. Try new things. They got all kinds of new-fangled products to get rid of pests. Ways to amend the soil. She won't hear nothing about it. Stubborn as sin, that one."

"What kinds of new things was Mr. Van Patten trying?" Angie said.

Fines told Angie that every year different insects blighted the crops.

"I never knew Brussels were so tasty," Fines said. "I mean why would you eat them when there's corn fields a quarter mile away?"

Angie had to agree with him. She'd never developed a taste for the "tiny cabbages."

Fines saw Van Patten right before lunch. When they parted ways, everything was normal. Except that Fines had a doctor's appointment in town that afternoon, so he was taking the rest of the day off.

"Bad ticker," he said. "I don't have cell service out here, so I never got the missus' messages, not that I could've done much."

"What time did you find him?"

"Shortly after sun up. It sure didn't look like Henry," Fines shook his head, "Never going to get that image out of my head."

Me either, Angie thought.

Other than the condition of the body, nothing out of the ordinary stood out in Fines' recollection. But he gave Angie the name of the company where Van Patten purchased his cutting-edge insecticides. That would be her next stop, but not before she settled one thing.

One hand on her car door she turned back to Fines.

"Mind if I ask you your age?" she said.

He laughed a big hearty sound. "Sixty-three. Hah! You thought I was younger." Fines winked at her. "Got my mom's good looks."

Angie winked. "You're a lucky man. Thanks for the help."

***

Pesticate's facility was an hour drive from town. Angie logged the destination into her phone assuring both perfect satellite directions and a formal check in with her Captain.

En route, she busied herself counting things because in the quiet moments, whenever she stopped actively doing something, the image of Henry's desiccated corpse popped into her mind, challenging even the basic task of driving. She passed thirty-four other vehicles on her drive...*What could've done that kind of damage to the body?* Four times, the two-lane highway opened up to passing lanes...*Were they looking at something natural or some sort of Satanic ritual?* She came to a stop at a red light before turning right onto Innovation Road, her destination close...*Even his eyes were shrunken, all intraocular fluid gone.* Angie focused on the odometer and watched it tick off the final mile as she passed corn fields.

Pesticate's facility was massive and sprawling. Several nondescript single-story monoliths lay one after the other, strewn like a child's carelessly thrown blocks. It looked like every industrial facility Angie had ever seen. Companies who valued profitability over aesthetics and this one's edifice was particularly ugly.

She'd called ahead, so it wasn't surprising when a tall man wearing a white lab coat over his blue button-down shirt and pressed khaki pants greeted her at the front entrance.

"Detective Ferguson," he said, thrusting out his hand. "You're shorter than I expected."

Angie hated it when men commented on her height. Especially tall ones, and this man towered over her. She judged him to be about six-two and buff. He looked like a man who spent a lot of time in the gym pressing weights. Angie nodded and ignored his extended appendage.

Nonplussed, he laughed then said, "I'm Operation Manager Craig Stanford."

"Mr. Stanford," she said. "Thank you for meeting me."

"Of course. We were sorry to hear about the farmer." Stanford frowned and shook his head. "Always a tragedy to lose one of our locals."

Especially, Angie thought, *when they're a customer.*

A gust of wind carried the sweet smell of corn pollen with it. Angie sneezed and felt a jolt of pain above her left eye. She pinched the bridge of her nose between her thumb and forefinger and wished she'd had a second cup of coffee or taken one of the prescription migraine pills she kept in her glove box.

"Early for corn," she said.

Stanford smiled. "My mother used to pinch her nose just like you're doing. Follow me, Detective."

He turned and took off at a fast pace away from the building where they'd met and angled down a dirt road. Dust kicked up from beneath his steps and Angie followed in his dirty wake until they came to a second building.

"We don't get many visitors out here," he said, opening the door using a key card on the lanyard around his neck.

Angie sneezed again and dabbed at her nose with a tissue she'd pulled from her pocket.

"Lots of security," she said. "What exactly is it that you do?"

She'd read over their official website before driving out, so she knew the basics of their pest control mission statement. At least, what they told the public.

"If I had a dollar..." he said and, holding the door open, he gestured for her to go inside. "As I said, I'm happy to answer questions, as long as they don't breach confidentiality. Our competitors would pay a fortune for inside information. But, honestly, I don't know how anything I can tell you would help in your investigation."

The door closed behind with a whoosh. Angie swore it felt like the air tightened around them.

"What the hell?" she said.

"Airlock," Craig said. "I don't even feel it anymore. Developing pesticides necessitates these types of precautions. Our labs are safe, but we're required by law to make sure that in the unlikely scenario of a laboratory breach, hazardous components..." Craig pointed to the posted hazardous waste sign. "...won't escape the building. Hence the airtight seals and pressure locks. As we edge away from toxic chemicals toward safer alternatives, we hope that one day, such safeties won't be necessary."

Angie waited in silence, wondering whether Craig's public relations spiel was memorized or off the cuff.

Craig nodded, then clapped his hands together like a child excited for a treat and said, "Come on."

He headed down a long corridor. The heels of Angie's shoes clicked against the polished linoleum floor as she followed, passing a dozen closed doors. When they came to the end of the hallway, Craig used his card key to open the final one. *What was he going to show her? What kinds of secret experiments lay inside?* Her pulse quickened as she stepped past him and into an ordinary looking conference room.

"Make yourself comfortable," Craig said, gesturing to one of the black plastic chairs that surrounded a long white table.

Angie took a seat as Craig strode to a bar on the far side of the room. While he grabbed a tray with a pitcher of water and a couple of glasses, Angie looked around. The walls, floors, and ceiling were all the same shade of white. She'd seen homier interrogation rooms. Craig situated himself directly across from her, setting the simple refreshment between them.

"May I?" He gestured to the water.

She nodded. He smiled and poured her a glass. His confidence and ease were agreeable enough, and he certainly wasn't acting like a man guilty of anything. But Angie wondered what lay behind his affable demeanor or all the doors they'd passed on their way to this room?

"So...," he said. "People die all the time. Heart attacks, strokes, all manner of deaths. Why's this one got you out on a goose chase?"

"Wild goose," Angie said, her voice catching.

Craig furrowed his brow. "I'm sorry?"

She cleared her throat and said, "The expression, it's wild goose chase."

Angie raised the glass of water. As it touched her lips, Craig's pupils dilated, raising alarms in her mind. Pesticate made pesticides. Something killed Henry Van Patten, maybe the company made a mistake, misjudged the strength of one of their products? If so, what lengths would they go to cover it up? Craig smiled at her. Water was an excellent vehicle transmitter. A single sip of this water might contain more than hydrogen and oxygen. She lowered the glass. He watched intently. Too intently.

"That's right, *wild* goose," Craig said. "Working for an industry like Pesticate, I forget anything wild remains." He winked, took a deep pull on his water and smacked his lips. "From our own wells. Best water around."

Something wasn't right about this man. The more time she spent with him, the more Angie felt like he was hiding something.

"You joke," she said. "Given the circumstances of Mr. Van Patten's death, I don't think there's anything funny about it."

He shrugged again. His "Aw-Shucks," mannerisms grew more

disingenuous by the minute. "I wouldn't know since you haven't told me about the circumstances."

There it was. Lie number one, and he'd walked right into it. Anton Fines mentioned that a representative from Pesticate paid him a visit before she'd been out to question him.

"Mr. Van Patten used some of your products in his fields. Do you have records that can tell us what he purchased?"

"Of course, we do."

Angie nodded. "Great. Can I access them?"

Craig Stanford shook his head. "Nope."

Angie interlaced her fingers and stared directly into the eyes of the man across from her. "What are you trying to hide, Mr. Stanford?"

He returned her gaze without blinking. "Nothing, Detective."

She lifted her water glass. She watched his pupils dilate again as she brought the rim closer to her mouth. *Some things just can't be hidden,* she thought, and, without taking a sip, returned the glass to the table.

"Mr. Fines could've been describing you when he told me about the man from Pesticate who came looking for answers."

"I have no idea what you're talking about."

"Seemed the most burning question wasn't about how the farmer might've died, but whether there'd been anything out of the ordinary about his body. So, you'll have to appreciate the fact that I think you're lying when you tell me you don't know anything."

"There's nothing in the water," he said.

"I never said there was." She reached across the table; she picked up his glass and in three big gulps finished it.

Stanford stared at her slack-jawed for a moment until interrupted by a buzz from his phone. He glanced at the screen and then answered. "Yes?" He listened while keeping watch on Angie the entire time. "Yes. Yes. I see. Yes." He hung up the phone. "It seems I'm to show you room 14." He stood. "This way."

Angie followed him back down the hallway until they stopped at a door that looked identical to all the rest. It lacked any identifying number.

"Room Fourteen?" she said.

"Yes, Detective," Stanford said, holding it open for her to pass.

Craig hit a switch, and halogen lights made the room as bright as the noonday sun. Angie squinted and threw a hand up to shield her eyes. Photophobia meant a migraine was definitely in the works, she needed to finish this interview, she could return later with a warrant and proper backup.

"Does it need to be so bright?" she said.

Turning back to Stanford, she saw that he'd donned sunglasses.

He smirked. "I wouldn't want you to miss anything. Welcome to where it all begins, Detective."

Floor to ceiling glass cages or aquariums, Angie wasn't sure what to call them, ran along two of the walls. Along the third, a long counter stood, covered with beakers, tubes, and a bunch of equipment Angie didn't recognize. A freestanding industrial sink took up the middle of the room. It had what looked like a shower head attached to a long arm and a drain directly in the floor.

"This a lab?" she said.

"Of a kind. We call it The Nursery." Craig gestured toward the glass. "Have a look."

She stepped closer to peer inside.

Insects. Hordes of insects and bugs.

It made sense. Pesticate's biggest sellers targeted vermin, that much was evident on their website. She didn't recognize the critters, but bugs weren't her specialty.

"Sap beetles," Craig said.

Angie jumped. While she'd been focusing on the fauna, Stanford crept up. His breath tickled the hairs on her neck, like little critter feet. She shivered.

He laughed. "Reaction of most people. They get the willies."

As if to prove to her he was fine with them, he opened an off-set door and stuck one of his arms up to his elbow inside. The beetles swarmed, quickly covering every bit of naked flesh.

"You ever feed them?" she asked.

"Watch this."

With the hand still outside the enclosure, he pressed a button. A mechanism released a single spritz of mist. The beetles scurried as far from Stanford's arm and the spray as they could manage in their confines.

"What is that?"

He removed his hand. "One of our projects. It's a deterrent." He licked his hand. "Non-toxic, safe for any crop."

"Targeting?"

"Whatever pest the farmer has difficulties with." Craig rubbed his hands together.

She peered into the next glass "cell." All these creatures held against their will to live out their lives in tiny clear torture chambers. Inside this one, she saw masses of undulating aphids. They were amassed on some food source, which Angie couldn't make out because the sheer volume of bugs was too great.

"I've never seen so many," she said.

"A Worship."

"What's that?"

"What we call a lot of aphids," Stanford said.

Angie rubbed her eyes. Flashing zig-zagging lights pulsed in her peripheral vision. Just a few more questions and she'd get out and to her car where she could pop Sumatriptan and get on the other side of this headache. She looked away from the aphids.

"The Worshipers—?"

"Just Worship, singular," he corrected.

"Worship. They receiving the same deterrent?"

"No. Different protocol. Two-fold really. We're attempting to create a sterile male—"

"Given the number in there, I'd say that's not working."

He waved his hand dismissing her. "Different strain than the ones in here. These ones are bred not to target plant juice." He turned toward the aphids.

The room closed in. Not really, Angie reminded herself. It was the auras, creating tunnel vision, but if it got bad enough, she'd be virtually blind. She opened her mouth to speak when the first wave of nausea hit her. She swallowed hard, willing herself to stay calm.

"I'm afraid I need to be back at the precinct," she said, reaching a hand to tap Craig's shoulder.

He startled, which was when she glimpsed that he'd reached into the aphid's prison to remove the remnants of their food. At least, that was what she thought he was doing, but everywhere she looked white spots danced, making it difficult to focus on anything. She thought he held something in his hand as he reached for her.

"You ask too many questions," he said, grabbing her with a sticky hand.

"I'm a detective. Release me before I charge you with assault."

"A right-handed, detective. There was never anything in the water, just a way to learn about you," he said.

Damn it, she thought. He's smarter than I thought. She needed to maintain control, pulling her weapon with her left hand, especially when she couldn't see well, would be a mistake.

He tightened his grip. Gone was any semblance of the glad-handing front man. Through her blurred vision, she thought the arm that held her pulsed with thousands of aphids. She felt them begin to crawl onto her. Stanford hadn't been holding anything in his hand except the Worship.

The first bites felt like tiny pinpricks. Struggling to pull free,

Angie lunged at him with her left hand, but he met her move, catching her wrist.

"Let me go!" she said, struggling to break free, but all her combat training was useless against a foe as big as Craig.

"The deterrent spray prevents the Worship from biting me. It doesn't make them flee, but it does seem to keep them from smelling the juices."

The Worship of aphids crawled faster than she'd imagined they could move, off of Craig's arms onto hers.

Craig laughed. "Their appetites surprised us."

More of the aphids moved up her arms. Angie felt them crawl beneath her shirt sleeves. This was how Van Patten died, she was sure of it.

"My Captain knows I'm here," she said.

"He'll be too late."

"They'll arrest you."

"No, they won't," Craig said. "The government has shown interest in our Worship. They want us to weaponize other insects as well. Already, one of their agents has taken over the farmer's autopsy. His official results will lay any questions to rest."

"A cover-up won't work."

She sucked in air. Her head pounded, but the pain of hundreds of tiny mouths sucking her flesh was excruciating. The aphids bit her neck and moved steadily toward her head. Her stomach roiled.

"Painful? I noticed your sensitivity to light, Detective. My mother used to get migraines. It's a bad one, isn't it?"

Angie heaved with no external warnings. The contents of her stomach covered Craig, who instinctually released his hold on her to cover his face with his arms. Angie fell forward, her knees crashing onto the floor.

"No!" Craig screamed, rushing to the sink to wash the vomit off.

Angie rubbed her hands together and then ran them back and forth against her arms, squashing as many aphids as she could. She would've rolled on the floor, but she knew she only had moments to make a move before Craig was back in the game. She turned her head until she could see him in the center of her remaining vision, pulled her weapon, and leveled it at his chest.

"I can't see, I can't see," he wailed, rinsing cold water over his face.

Excellent, Angie thought, taking a few steps closer. The bites continued to punish her flesh, but she held her revolver with both hands.

"Welcome to my world," she said. "At least I've got some practice being blind."

Craig lifted his gaze, water streamed from his face. Though he squinted, she knew he saw her gun.

"Keep your hands where I can see them and move away from the sink."

Craig stepped away. Keeping her gun trained on Craig, she put the phone on the counter, hit speed dial, and as the call went through, she began to wash as many of the aphids off her body as she could one arm at a time.

"Ferguson?" her Captain's voice clear through the phone's speaker. "You okay?"

By the time her backup arrived, she'd moved Craig outside, taken her prescription, and was starting to feel better. At least her head. Her skin felt like she'd suffered a bad sunburn, and an occasional prick told her she hadn't killed all of the Worship yet.

A row of bystanders stood outside the facility watching as Angie led Craig to the squad car. Angie was sure that the CEO and other corporate heads were among them. No doubt plotting their next move.

She covered Craig's head as she shoved him into the back seat.

He smirked. "I'll be out before sunset."

"We'll see," Angie said.

"You threw up on me," he said. "If that hadn't happened, this ending would've been different."

"I call it a Cavalry of Puke," she said.

"Funny."

"I think so," Angie said, "Tell me something. I assume lots of farms received your product. Why'd the aphids target Van Patten?"

Craig Stanford gave her a look that made her wish she'd stayed in bed that day. Then he started to laugh.

"That's your question? I have no idea. You'll have to ask the Worship."

"Asshat," she said and, slamming the door, she hit the top of the roof twice. Once to say he was inside and once for good luck.

She watched along with the other spectators as the squad car pulled away.

When it disappeared from sight, Pesticate's troops headed back inside to continue creating their monsters of destruction. But wasn't that the bottom line with monsters, Angie thought? Weren't they by definition destructive? Angie pushed up her shirt sleeves. A single aphid sucked greedily near her elbow. Tiny monster. She smacked it dead.

Dead Katherine

Victoria Zelvin

Victoria Zelvin is a writer living and
working in Washington D.C. Her
short fiction has previously appeared
in publications from Daily Science
Fiction, Shoreline of Infinity, Mason
Jar Press, and OutWrite DC among
others. She has a day job in ocean
conservation. For more please visit:
www.victoriazelvin.com

The dust blew through her hair as the outlaw surveyed the carnage around her, dim in the shadow of the oncoming dust storm. She stood among the scattered dead like a commemorative monument erected after the fact. Katherine hadn't killed them, except that she had, her body had, the body that was Dead Katherine and the body that she shared with Talia. That wasn't to say that Katherine wouldn't have killed them of her own accord—she would have, she had been trying to, only to find it quite suddenly over before she'd really started.

"What happened?" Katherine asked, when she'd found her own voice again. Her throat was as thick with coarse sand as the bodies collecting it at her feet.

They fired in a line when you crested the hill. You were hit a half dozen times. I took over.

Talia's voice was like a soft wind, making the hairs on the back of Katherine's neck stand up. When Talia took over, her vision went the purple color of a bruise around the edges and she invariably lost track of time. Not quite lost control of herself, not entirely. It was more like being close to blackout drunk—still somewhere in there, but sloppy, feeling like swimming upstream, half fighting as she surrendered her body over to someone else, half blissfully relieved to be along for the ride. It was hard to piece together after.

Being shot a half dozen times also didn't help. Her body felt fine, a little stiff maybe, but her head was a fog that thoughts had to wade through to get to the forefront of her brain. Was it just her, or was this one worse?

Will they be getting up? It had been long enough that Katherine was starting to be annoyed with herself for instinctively trying to look for the ghostly alien, like Talia was actually speaking from somewhere over her left shoulder instead of her own mind.

Katherine nudged a nearby man's calf with the tip of her boot, like that was what she always intended instead of looking for ghosts. "Nah, probably not," she said, real quiet. While Talia got to be a wind, Katherine had to actually speak aloud to respond.

Bit unfair, that, but that was their current arrangement in a nutshell.

"Excuse me, miss?"

The voice behind her made her jump, whirling around. She would have had a revolver up and ready to fire from her hip had there actually been one in the holster. "Dammit, where's my gun?" she muttered out of the corner of her mouth.

Probably among the bodies.

Anxiety crouched on her chest and dug in the spurs as she stared at the woman, one hand up in a gesture of no ill intent. The woman wore a dress made out of flour sacks with rough edges, sewn patchwork, like Frankenstein. She raised her hands in turn. She even made a pretty good show of painting on a smile right after she'd checked Katherine's right arm. There was no blue armband overtop her jacket like Dawes' men had, pretending they were the law in the Dust.

Behind the woman was a caravan of four wagons, but more like three and a half if she wasn't being generous. Not enough to arrange into a horseshoe, even if they'd had time to try. Bullet holes pockmarked the worn canvas stretched over the top, and splintered in some of the siding.

"You folks alright?" Katherine asked, drawl thicker than it had been talking to herself. The woman was wearing a hat fit for a cowboy, and it pulled at some long atrophied part of Katherine's brain that yearned to connect with someone else.

"Yes," the woman said, a little too quickly. She had, Katherine was a little disappointed to learn, no real drawl to speak of. Northeast accent. "Oh, thank you. Thank you miss."

The woman's gratitude curdled in her gut, so much so she felt like she was fighting the urge to retch. *There's more of them, peering from around the wagons,* Talia said, and indeed there were. Rail thin people, gaunt faces, peering around from behind axles and oxen. Most were pinkish red, despite the wide brimmed, sensible hats and long sleeves they wore. *We should ask why they ran away instead of helping.*

Katherine didn't have the freedom to tell Talia exactly why these people had done the right thing by getting the hell out of the way of the shooting, especially with kids among them, and not look like a madwoman. "You work for Dawes?" she asked instead, feeling Talia recede into a testy silence like she did when she was ignored.

That stopped the woman up short. She glanced into the wagon, and then back at Katherine. "We—I mean, we've been that way. Did some day's work, when work was offered..."

"Hearing there's a fair bit these days," Katherine said. "But here's you heading in the other direction."

Silence stretched between them. Anxiety dug that spur a little deeper into her ribcage. She kept looking behind the woman for why, but only too large eyes stuck in gaunt faces stared back. Some of these people were several steps past sun-kissed, faces peeling in thin white strips. Work in the sun? Was Dawes shifting the work outside? Last Katherine and Talia had heard he was stuck in some mine somewhere.

"Afraid I can only offer you words in gratitude, miss," the woman said, entirely misreading her wandering eyes.

Katherine waved a hand. "Where you folks coming from?"

"East a ways. Originally come outta Connecticut."

Katherine let out a low whistle. She had thought there wasn't much of Connecticut left these days to flee from. She cast a look behind her again, this time her eyes lingering on a pair of boots attached to a thin body laid up in the back of the wagon. The woman traced her eyes, then sighed. When she spoke next, her eyes were downcast. "My husband...worked the mines a spell, until his...he was sick already, ma'am, wasn't his fault he dropped that detonator. He's suffering too—his, his arm—"

Katherine moved forward in a burst of speed too quick for the woman to intercept. If she'd tried, she would have bounced off Katherine like she'd hit a brick wall—another perk of fusing with Talia. It was also the reason she yanked the canvas cover right off of where it had been securely tied, tearing almost all the way up to the top. She grimaced, but pushed it aside in favor of looking at the man on the wagon floor.

His face was bright red and peeling, like he'd been laying

directly in the sun instead of in the shade, and beads of sweat dotted his forehead. He was missing his left arm, bloodied bandages wrapped tight to the stump. A girl child of about four sat at his head, bright pink in the face and big, wide brown eyes that seemed quite unfairly reflective.

Katherine fell into that gaze, enough that it took her a moment to notice the woman was at her side, lips working open, then shut, then open. When she found her voice, it was timid. "You're her, aren't you? Dead Katherine. The—you don't look much like you're dead."

A muscle popped in her temple. "Thanks, I try."

"He's terrified of you."

Dawes. Katherine reached forward, touching the tip of the man's boot, then his leg. Something was stung at her like she'd rubbed a brush's bristle. "Glad I'm getting his attention."

That explained why he was after these folks. A shame, as Katherine was hoping to find an armory, a messenger, something... these folks were refugee workers that accidentally blew up a part of his mine. Like any good mob boss, Dawes had just been cleaning up shop by sending those riders to stop them from spreading word to stay away or giving out the secret of his location.

"More than that," the woman said, breathless. Now that the tap had been turned on, she was spilling everywhere. Nerves, Katherine suspected, finally frayed and unleashed on the first new person who stopped long enough. "I've never seen such a fortress. He won't leave it, not until someone brings him your head."

"Hope he's built that fortress real nice and claustrophobic like," Katherine replied, brightly. She even affixed a humorless smile to her face.

Hope he suffocates in it, added Talia. It made the corners of Katherine's lips twitch that much further up.

"What did he do to you?"

Katherine sobered quickly, closing down any false camaraderie as she shut the tent flap. She'd already saved these people, she owed them no more of her concern. She jammed a hand into her jacket pocket and produced a dusty tablet. It came to life with a hard press of the button by her knuckle, a dim map appearing under the dusty screen. She held it out to the woman. "I need you to point out real clear on this map where his aboveground operation is. I know he's burrowed deep, but every mine has an entry somewhere. Tell me where, I'll show you safe haven to bunker down that storm before you really get gone."

The woman's casual demeanor stiffened. She looked her down once, then trailed slowly back up again. "Would you tell us even if I said I didn't know?"

There was a test there. She didn't need Talia's quick warning buzz to know it. Stand firm or act gentle? Be Dawes or Robin Hood? Katherine weighed the answer, worrying her tongue at her teeth. When she spoke, it was in a lowered, self-righteous tone. "Ride towards the sun three miles, there's a town called New Haven that'll take you in."

There was silence but for the rustle of the wind through the dust. But then, slowly, as if Katherine had offered her a loaded gun, she took it. She scrolled for a second, her brows furrowed tight, before pressing a finger to the screen and dropping a pin at the base of a river in a valley nestled between three mountains.

Katherine took it back without a word. She turned and took one heavy step away, and meant to take more, if she could find the strength to lift her boot. Concern itched at her, like the gritty way the fingertips that had touched the man tingled still. Another sunburned child poked his cartoonish eyes around the side of the wagon.

Katherine's mouth tasted bitter as she walked away.

***

The white, nickel-plated revolver was hiding under the sixth body she pushed over with the tip of her boot. The man appeared to have been shot, but he also had a purpling bruise over the side of his face. "What, did you throw it at him?" Katherine muttered, crouching down to pick her weapon up from the dirt and swatting some of the dust off the side.

It popped, causing damage to you. I got rid of it before it got too bad.

Katherine looked down at her hand, noticing for the first time the shiny patch of skin over the knuckle of her thumb, like she'd had a burn there. Inspection of the revolver showed it was a little charred, but it was when she popped the barrel out that she truly saw what had happened. "Christ," she mumbled, prodding the shrapnel stuck in one of the chambers. It poked her finger and made blood begin to well out for the few seconds before Talia sighed and the wound began to close in a haze of purple. The burn went with it, and a twist started to turn up against her temple. Migraines when Talia used her unnatural powers were also part of the package deal, as helpful as the healing had been to date.

Katherine pouted, lips pursed. "One of us double loaded it."

The gun had exploded. One of them had stuffed in a cap and power, then someone had come along behind and loaded another cap and powder. The one in the back had exploded in a manner that Katherine was trying not to think might've blown off her hand if Talia hadn't been in control, hadn't reacted to a millisecond's pain.

There was still powder in there. If she fired that chamber, the ball would lodge somewhere unpleasant in the barrel, and her hand really would come off.

Blowing out muttered, nonsensical swears under her breath, Katherine flipped the chamber around to reload the others. She didn't have time to fix it, not if she meant to make the mines before the storm. She was just going to have to start remembering to count to five.

Why not take one of theirs?

"I like this one."

Her mind's eye image of Talia was making a face. Katherine imagined her pursing her lips together, but this was always accompanied by the reminder she had no guarantee Talia even had lips. Katherine had never seen the passenger in her mind. *It's defective...or is this one of those 'shut up, ghost' human moments?*

"It's one of those moments, though for the record I said that one time and I apologized."

And yet I have not forgotten it.

"Yeah, noticed that."

Katherine straightened up, tugging her vest back down so it rested more over her hips. She'd lost weight since she'd died, and now all her clothes felt as ill-fitting as her new name. She pulled her hat down a little further on her face as the wind kicked up some dust, eyes on the big storm brewing on the horizon.

***

They ran quick and hard, Talia taking control of her body to speed the journey. For all that Katherine and Talia had been circling these lands—the whole 7000 acres of it that belonged to William Dawes, and he wasn't going to let anyone forget it, nevermind it was near valueless so long as the dust storms persisted—he'd holed up and built his mines not two miles away from the valley they'd been riding through for weeks. This could have been good planning, that all that circling they'd done had paid off and put them in the path of a caravan that needed help at the right moment and could point them the last few paces to their direction, but it stank of pure dumb luck enough that Katherine was in a bad mood when she laid down on the bluff overhang to spy on his bustling operation. It wasn't much above ground—some dumping ground, a building or two, a long road with wagons moving to and from—but there was a big, obvious hole in the side of the mountain. She could see tents peeking out there, workers taking shelter in the slope of the cavern. There were walls up, gates, guarded. Towers filled with armed men.

Souring her mood further was the toll travel took on her since Talia joined her. Was she clearing vast distances like a streaking purple wind, careless of obstacles in her path? Yes. Did that effort make it feel like someone was determinedly jabbing ice picks into the tops of her eyes? Also, yes.

"How could we have missed this?" she muttered into her binoculars, for the eighth time that hour.

That is derivative. Focus please. And stop squirming so much.

She squirmed a little bit more, harder, just to be contrary. Talia settled into a testy silence. That was out of character, though admittedly Katherine didn't know as much as she probably should about her companion, though it wasn't as though Katherine had been an open book about her life either. The silence felt heavier than normal, though, and Katherine couldn't let it stand.

"Are you going to tell me what wedged that stick up your butt?"

Talia made a little noise that was either *hmrph* or a rude word. Katherine stayed quiet until they both came to the understanding that either Talia spoke about what was bothering her or let the conversation die. Katherine was starting to bet on the latter winning out when Talia finally was out with it. *It is...getting harder to heal you. To do this.*

"Okay," Katherine said, slow. "Something I can do to help?"

We need to move. I am not supposed to be incorporeal for so long. There's some...it would look like a vial of liquid to you. I need to absorb some of it.

"And something bad happens if you don't?"

It's like dying of thirst.

"Alright," Katherine said. She felt like she was grasping at straws. This was the first non-human being (*alien*, as Talia kept calling herself) that Katherine had shared her head with, and no one had bothered to give her a guidebook. "You think Dawes has your ship at his mines, there's the mines. Let's get some more intel. Assuming it gets worse the more you use your juice, so meantime, don't take over and don't heal me if you don't have to. Agreed?"

If you were less reckless with your body, I wouldn't have to heal you so much, Talia retorted, and Katherine didn't have a good comeback to retaliate with. Being with Talia had made her feel more than a little immortal.

***

As the storm was starting to swallow the setting sun, they took down a scout.

The sunburned boy was still breathing in the dim light, but he seemed dreadfully aware of how likely he'd not see the rising moon. There had been a lot of huffing and puffing and tears and not much coherence, but he'd given up a tablet and rubbed his wrists raw on the rope she'd tied him with. He was working his way around to having an actual thought, voice trembling a bit as he started to speak."You're her, aren't you?" Katherine puffed up as he searched for the words, jutting her chin up just a bit. "The...he calls you She-Demon."

Katherine made a face. "Can't even call me by the right name, no, has to make up his own name." She paused only long enough to deflate, a heavy breath pushing from her lips. "Yeah, yeah, I'm the—whatever. They call me a lot of things."

But I like Dead Katherine, Talia supplied. That made her smile, just a little.

The boy was still puffed up. "You're not going to get away with what you're doing to him!"

His men act like thugs, and you're the villain for stopping them? I do not understand this planet.

Maybe it was cruel to lean over him, close enough that he flinched, but damn if it didn't feel good. "I was going and he chased me down. Now all of a sudden he don't want me here?"

The boy didn't have a retort. Katherine stood up and let him be, moving away a little to press at the tablet she'd taken off him. An electronic map, inside his little fortress. Entrances. Guard posts.

The mine. And, most importantly, a blocked-off white square of space labeled only 'SALVAGE'.

"What do you think?"

Katherine imagined Talia pressing fingers to her lips as she thought. Did Talia have fingers? Must have, how'd she grip things otherwise? In her mind's eye, Talia was very human, but she easily probably wasn't. *It's probably legitimate,* Talia said, which was hardly helpful. *We should use this to get inside.*

"I agree," Katherine said pointedly. "I was more asking for thoughts about how we do that."

Oh, Talia said. After a beat, she added: *I don't know.*

"Thanks," Katherine grunted out, standing. Her thighs ached from so long on horseback and trembled under her. Crouching had been a mistake. Under her, the scout looked like he was waging a debate with himself as to whether or not to ask about her talking to nothing. With a look up and down, she could see him decide not to mention it like he was physically closing a door.

He instead turned to something more practical. "Are you...going to kill me?"

We likely should. He'll tell everyone that we are coming.

"...may not be the worst thing," Katherine mumbled.

"What?" His voice was sharp. He was coiling in on himself like a snake, not that she expected his strike to be very hard.

"Nothin'," she said. She slipped her knife from her belt, then leaned in. He tensed, started to babble, but all she did was cut the ropes with one quick swipe. Before she backed away she yanked his blue armband off in a single rough motion, balling it up tight in her fist. "Do yourself a favor and don't be on the west gate come sundown, because that's where Dawes will get what's coming to him."

He was frozen for a moment, not daring to move. His eyes were as wide as a doe's, fixed on her.Then, quick as he could, he scrambled away, noisily kicking rocks and scattering dust as he raced away on four limbs at first and then on two.

Was that wise?

"Dunno." Katherine affixed the blue band over her left bicep, pressing her tongue against her teeth distastefully. "Let's see if they fall for it."

***

Night and the storm overhead darkened the sky as the group of guards on the west gate tripled, steadily working the way up to quadrupled. In the middle of it all was their scout, gesticulating and seeming to direct the flow, a small group of official-looking older types around him. Couldn't hear what he was saying from where Katherine had set up her overwatch, but it looked like the kid's number had gone up among the veterans for having survived the she-demon. Katherine smiled to herself as she lowered her binoculars. "Good for you kid, get yourself a promotion."

What?

"Nothin'."

She was tucked into a small blind, down as close as she dared to one of the gates. The wind was picking up, the storm almost upon them. She'd seen sunburned workers start to erect defenses, but they were lackluster. They weren't moving quickly enough.

Apathy or exhaustion? Katherine couldn't decide. Regardless, when the dust storm swallowed the camp like a child pouring a bucket of water over an anthill, there was a hole enough that she could slip right through that gate. In the swirling dust she was an anonymous shape—blue armband, cowboy hat, bandana tied over her face to breathe, who was to say she didn't belong? After all those weeks of aimless wandering, she walked right into the camp, through what amounted to be the front door, and down the entrance to the mines without so much as a how-do-you-do from anyone who should have stopped her.

The night shifted from cool to chilled the deeper she went, the memorized map burned into her mind's eye. Something else burned too, though, itching at her. She'd only been climbing down, far enough now she had hit winding hallways of stone instead of tent villages, when she noticed her skin was turning a little pinkish.

There's radiation down here, Talia hissed, like it was something Katherine ought to understand like the sun shining. *Something's happened to the power source. Spend long enough around it and it burns you from the inside out. Invisible.*

Katherine felt a shiver down her spine. A lot of knowledge had been lost when the old world ended. Some things reverted back if they already had the template for survival, and hundreds of years down the line didn't make the new Dust Bowl West any easier to traverse on horseback or on a desperate wooden wagon than it had been back when it was first flooded with those seeking their manifest destiny, no matter the harm. The concept of radiation was something that had been largely lost. For Katherine, it conjured a cartoonish vision of a skull and crossbones flag. Poison, at best, dangerous, stay away, the reason why lost while the warning survived.

But burning from the inside out. That was specific, and tugged on a memory. "Those people. They weren't sunburned."

They likely have radiation poisoning. Especially if, as they said, he was keeping people down here for days at a time.

"That's—" Katherine stopped abruptly, slamming her back against the far wall. Voices, in the next room. She couldn't quite make out what they were saying, but she knew one tone above the others. Angling her head, she peered around the corner, and her whole world tilted slightly left.

There, among two others, was Dawes. Cowboy hat on his head. Stupid blue band around his bicep. For a few blinks she didn't see him, not there. She saw him walking down the main road to town, strutting like he owned the place. Saw him in her parent's General Store, making gestures in her direction, always lingering close enough that her father came out from the back to man the counter. Saw his expression when she told him no, she wasn't interested, no thank you. Saw him there, outlined by the fire of the store. Saw him with the night sky above him, gun in his hand, illuminated by the streak of purple across the sky and the explosion not far off. Remembered, like a whisper, Talia's voice after the echo of his gunshot had faded, a promise and a plea and the start of a partnership: *hey, please, I don't want to die either.*

Talia's hate of him was only by osmosis, really, but there was plenty of bile in her voice when she spoke.

My ship, Talia said. Katherine only barely noticed now it was behind Dawes, dead like the metal buildings of the old world, surrounded by half a cave in. *The power core, it's gone, it's gone, the—I need it, I need to go check.*

"Do it," Katherine whispered. If she was honest she'd say she'd expected more of a fight, but Talia was gone with a physical *whoosh* that left Katherine sagging a bit against the wall. The absence of her after so long with her was jarring.

Maybe she should have stayed still, then. Waited here for Talia to return, hoped no one noticed her, hide. But being with Talia had given her confidence, and it had taught her something. Standing there, Dawes didn't look like a boogeyman. He just looked like a man.

And she'd killed plenty of those recently.

She popped up, pistol in hand. The man to Dawes' right was looking at her, so she shot him first, two quick pops in the chest. The other man caught a shot in the head. By the time Dawes turned, gun in hand, held low at his hip, they were dropping.

Katherine shot Dawes square in the chest. He shot her in the gut, low by her hip. The pain barely registered, and she made to shoot him again when he burst forward. Too fast. In a streak of purple.

Her brain barely had time to register what she was seeing. He slapped his hand out, knocking the gun from hers, and then rocking the hand backwards, backhanding her with enough force to drop her to the ground. Pain starburst suddenly through her side, nerves catching up, and in a daze she was back to where he'd had her the first time he'd drawn a gun on her.

Flat on her back, staring up at him over the barrel of his gun.

Her ears were ringing. Dawes was smiling, glowing bright purple.

"Katherine, dear!" His voice boomed, echoing through the space. "You shouldn't have! Hold that thought. There's something I want to show you." He seemed to mean that too, holstering his gun and moving back to the ramp, utterly ignoring the bodies of his compatriots and the fact she was bleeding out on the dusty floor.

The feeling of having been murdered was as real as grains of sand between her fingers—coarse, uncomfortable, but unshakable. Katherine growled out, angry, unwilling to let him do it a second time. She could see the glint of her gun across the way. Dawes was bent over the side of the ship, digging for something. Katherine pressed one hand over her leaking side and started to move. He didn't stand to stop her. It was only after her long, agonized crawl to the gun that she realized she had no plan. By her count she had one bullet left, one real bullet, and that wasn't enough, not if he was like her.

She was still frozen, hand wrapped around the handle, when she felt a rush of adrenaline, and the room took on a purplish tint.

I'm here. Talia's voice was a cooling breeze across her feverishly hot mind. *I can—we can take him. Get up.*

Katherine almost did it. Without question, she almost lifted herself up and rounded on him with the pistol, filled with Talia's conviction that they could and must kill him. But, something held her down for just a split second long enough to remember why she hadn't tried that already.

If they killed Dawes, they'd never know what he'd done with the ship's core, and Talia...

One real bullet left.

"You're not here," she whispered. She didn't know if Dawes was still paying her much mind, so she tried to sound suitably heartbroken just in case he was listening.

I am, Katherine. The power cell's gone, but I'm here.

"No," Katherine whispered, more forcefully. "You're not."

Pistol tight in her hand, she forced herself to stand on shaky, wobbly knees. A glance over her shoulder showed he was there, bent over some rubble, back to her. She took one shuffling step toward him and then another. The hole in her gut was leaking hot blood against her fingers, not deterred in the slightest by the painful pressure of her hand. Katherine pressed anyway. She pressed even though her breathing was short and scraping, even though her steps were slow and staggering. Strength bled from her as sure as hot blood, leaking from every part of her body except her gun arm. That didn't shake as she lifted her pistol, and cocked it.

"Reach for the sky."

Dawes froze. Turned like his body instinctively knew what it had heard even as his brain tried to reject it. A slow, stuttering movement, and regardless of if he believed it or not when he faced her, there was a muzzle aimed between his eyes. She pressed it to his forehead, just in case he needed any help remembering it was a loaded gun.

"I said," Katherine rasped. "Reach for the—"

Too fast, Dawes surged forward. She squeezed the trigger, but the bullet ricocheted off the cave wall and against the ship's hull. He elbowed her hard in the stomach, and she went down again. In an instant their positions were reversed—he had the gun pressed to her forehead, not noticing or not caring how she flinched to feel the hot metal there.

"You dumb bitch," he said. "You never did know what was good for you."

She could feel Talia bristling inside her. Katherine willed her to stand down, shut up, even as she let her voice shake a bit as she spoke. "And you know exactly what's good for everyone, is that it?"

He pressed the gun more firmly forward. Katherine winced, even as her eyes were filled with long unspent rage. Looking at him head on hurt her eyes, the brightness of whatever he was glowing with searing into her. "This is going to help me make a dynasty." His eyes flashed, purple to white. Katherine had a bit of a horrified realization that this might've been what she looked like when Talia took over. "You could have been a part of that, if you weren't so stuck up."

"What?" Katherine asked, quick. "What's going to help you build a dynasty?"

He swung his free arm out, over to the ship. "It was filled with power you can't imagine," he said. "And now, all of that is inside me. All of it."

He can't possibly mean that literally, can he?

Katherine's eyes dipped down to his stomach, then back up. "Did you...drink a vial of mystery glowing liquid from space?"

His eyes flashed. "It's from the heavens!"

So, yes.

Katherine nodded, just a little bit, just for Talia, but Dawes took it as for him. He pressed the pistol forward enough to knock her head back, then took several steps back, keeping the barrel leveled at her head as he spread his other arm in a flourish. "Last chance, Katherine," he said. She feared from the tone of his voice that he was trying to be sincere. "Join me, convince me you're sorry, or I blow your head off right here."

"Go to hell."

Dawes squeezed the trigger. For a moment, nothing happened. Then there was a fizzle, like the lead to a firework, and with a ear-ringing pop the nickel plated revolver exploded. In just a blink to protect her eyes, Katherine missed the transition of the explosion.

Dawes had a hand and a revolver, blink, and he had neither.

Eyes wide as saucers, Dawes sank to his knees, other hand coming to wrap tight around his stump. He wasn't bleeding, not yet, his body as shocked by the turn of events as Katherine was. From within the stump a purple light started to shine, the same tint as Talia. It grew no larger than a small polished stone before Katherine's hand snapped out to grab his stump—no, not Katherine's, *Talia's*.

Katherine was aware of being on her feet without transition. Angling Dawes down by his forearm, pushing him to his knees. "*You,*" Talia said, with Katherine's voice. "*Should not have ingested that.*"

There was a swell of purple light—bright this time instead of dull, but shining as a flare. It made spots dance over vision, and when she blinked rapidly to clear them there were tears on her face. The whole cavern was glowing, vibrant purple and there where Dawes had been was another figure. Shimmering, translucent.

"Talia," she breathed.

The woman looked at her. Or, Katherine thought she did. There was no face, only a feeling. She was ghostly as ever. Katherine stumbled back half a step, strength starting to fail her, but Talia lifted an appendage, not quite an arm but more like the tendril of a jellyfish, and in another little burst of light the pain from her side was gone. She felt as rested as if she'd slept for hours. Her head felt clearer, enough to notice the ship, Talia's ship, had the same shimmering material around it now, glowing inside out and reflecting outward like a forcefield.

Down the hall, angry voices echoed. Talia looked at Katherine. Katherine looked at Talia.

"Go," Katherine whispered. She reached up a hand, but the air was too heavy between them, and she couldn't close the distance. Couldn't touch her. "Go, now's your chance."

Talia squirmed. Opened her mouth, shut it. It felt like she pulled the air from Katherine's lungs as she turned away, and glided up the ramp, toward the doorway bathed in light.

The angry voices were getting louder.

Katherine should go. She knew she should go, but she was rooted to the spot, unable to look away from Talia.

Talia turned back before she got to the doorway. Held a hand down the ramp for her. "Come with me." An offer, not a question.

Katherine had rocked forward automatically before realizing she ought to maybe pause. To ask questions, to think through the implications of what the alien was offering. But she could only come up with one question. "Will you stay with me?"

She was so unused to it that she couldn't identify the expression across Talia's face, except to say that it was vulnerable. "I always want to," she whispered, voice as gentle as a soft wind.

Katherine didn't hesitate again. She reached out and squeezed the hand that solidified beneath her. She let Talia pull her into the spaceship.

The Space Beyond Cubicle Twenty-Nine

Chelsea Sutton

Chelsea Sutton writes weird fiction, plays and films. She was a 2016 PEN America Emerging Voices Fellow and is member of the Clarion UCSD 2020/21 class. She has just finished her first short story collection, Curious Monsters, which was the runner-Up for the 2018 Madeline P. Plonsker Emerging Writers Residency Prize. Her writing has appeared in The Rattling Wall, Bourbon Penn, The Texas Observer, The Exposition Review, LA Review of Books, Cosmonaut Avenue and Pithead Chapel, and is forthcoming in Craft Literary, Sequestrum, and F(r)iction. Chelseasutton.com

Ted Jenkins is going to space.

He marches into the office on a Tuesday morning in full astronaut attire and helmet and tells this to Mr. Gardner, the Executive Director of Earth Interface Publishing, who's halfway through his onion bagel.

Everyone is going to space these days. Rising like steam from boiling water.

Lucy is watching through the skewed blinds of Mr. Gardner's office. Three hours after Lois—Mr. Gardner's long-term assistant—left, Mr. Gardner opened the blinds and they got stuck like that, diagonal and wrapped around themselves. Every day since, each time someone shows up in Mr. Gardner's office dressed as an astronaut—and they do, every day—Lucy sits at this window and draws on the glass with a sharpie, an interconnected, large tableau: a cornfield with each lost employee staring up at the skies in various positions of worship, as Lucy has seen in old paintings of people bowing down to angels. For Ted, she draws a flying saucer hovering above him.

Of course, there are no angels. No aliens. Only the Humans who appeared from the skies.

A dollop of cream cheese splats onto Mr. Gardner's tie as he watches Ted rant about space. Ted's new uniform is silver and form fitting, making him look like a giant, excitable bullet. Lucy misses his lightly patterned collared shirts—blue stripes and wagon wheels and micro pigs rolling in micro-mud puddles and palm trees against a multitude of orange suns. This is not his style at all.

Marcia the copywriter (cubicle twenty) and Dave the photographer (cubicle 5) stand beside Lucy, watching Ted gesture and nearly rip his suit in the passion of it all. Marcia comments that the depiction of Lois is far too skinny in Lucy's drawing. Dave the photographer mentions that the corn in her cornfield drawing is too short or the people are too tall, that cornfields don't work that way, the way she is drawing it—bending and curling around the feet and legs and bellies of the people. *Has it really been that long since you saw corn?* Dave the photographer cocks his head and glances at Marcia the copywriter, who is slurping her Greek yogurt and nodding along. *Watch a movie sometime. Read a book. Do your research if you're going to draw a cornfield right.*

Lucy is nodding and uh-huh-ing but not listening to them. A nano earphone is attached to her left ear, tucked out of sight, pumping in music (today it is mostly James Brown and Betty Davis). After she got sick and eight months of treatments left scratching reverberation and faraway screaming echoing in her mind, day in and day out, the music is the only thing that helps her focus. The real benefit being that it was much easier to drown out Marica the copywriter and Dave the photographer.

Mr. Gardner has never mentioned the drawings to Lucy.

Ted is saying something about going to space and being a hero. *The Humans have brought hope. The Humans have brought the future.* Everyone always says the same thing. Speeches speckled with phrases from the visitations by the Humans, who looked like us, like humans, only grander, arriving in meticulously tailored suits with silver details, sharp muscles in a towering frames, smiles so wide and welcoming it seemed they had more teeth than needed, that the edges of their lips stretched to their ears and wrapped around their heads.

Ted gives a full-fledged quitting speech for a good five minutes straight and never realizes that his helmet is still on and Mr. Gardner can't hear a word he's saying.

But he doesn't need to.

Ted catches Lucy's eye through the window of Mr. Gardner's office. And he smiles—an unnaturally large smile.

It started almost two years ago, as storms raged and droughts hissed and the earth started cracking along its skin, and the workload of Earth Interface Publishing hit a new stride. Every new problem needed its own journal, articles, editors, photographers, graphic designers, and Mr. Gardner ordered a new set of storm doors for his house in the suburbs (the actual ordering was done by Lois, of course).

Humans appeared from space in large ships similar to old sci-fi shows—as if they designed their flying saucers from their own childhood comic books and cartoons, from daydreams in fifth grade science class. They weren't aliens, they told the world. They were human from the future—Humans with a capital H, upgraded, newly improved—here to save us from ourselves because *the earth is dying, if you hadn't noticed.* It was in their own best interest: helping humans escape the planet would guarantee their own existence in the future. It was a win-win deal, saving their great-great grandparents, and so forth. Loopy time travel things Lucy didn't understand. She'd sit for hours in her studio apartment, watching the press conferences, the speeches, images of the Humans visiting hospitals and movie studios and factories and talking with folks, spreading the good word of the Human race's future. Lucy wondered what it meant to be saved from oneself. What does it look like? Was it like those old action movies, someone dangling from a skyscraper by one hand, watching themselves standing over them, stomping on their fingers, one by one? Lucy would sketch it out in her notebook, people being saved from themselves. And when she ran out of paper, she'd draw on the walls, until her entire apartment was covered, and then the hallway, and her car, and her cubicle.

The Humans appeared on television, but not in public right away. First, it was the commercials.

A constant loop of rockets zooming to space. A priest, a nurse, a school teacher, a mother, a father. Your neighbor. An entire office of cubicle workers. Leaving the Earth with the Humans. Following their destinies. Being saved from themselves.

Regular commercials for beer and diapers and eyeliner and tampons were gone. Even those long-form commercials for pills with some guy spitting out a list of side effects that seem far worse than whatever problem the person had to begin with. Even those. Lucy missed those most of all.

Lucy saw the first commercial with Ted. She'd just made them a dinner of roast beef and mashed potatoes and crushed cheese puffs and had sat down to watch reruns of one of those conspiracy shows with the FBI agent who believes in aliens and the one who thinks it's a crock.

Ted and Lucy laughed at the commercials at first, but another five appeared within the hour, and Ted got a faraway taste in his breath and a rubbery cold when he touched Lucy's skin. Lucy worried that maybe he was thinking of his wife or his son at home, that maybe he was finally regretting the affair, but he wasn't looking at the clock or his phone or even out the window. Instead he looked up, as if through the ceiling, his lip curling slightly at the corner.

Soon the commercials only ran between reruns because all the television shows stopped shooting. And then, only the commercials. No reruns. No stories at all.

The doctors called it a spiral tumor, for lack of a better term. They made it up while in the breakroom, waiting for toaster strudel to warm up.

They told Lucy it was a tumor but not quite, cancer but not quite, something else maybe, a spiraling linking of cells twirling like ballerinas through her organs, not really killing her yet but maybe that's why she can't focus that well, maybe that's why she's hearing that rumbling and far-off screaming at night sometimes, and maybe we should try a few experimental things. *A new kind of radiation*, they said. *A couple hours a day. We're sure your boss will understand.*

On the walks back to the office, Lucy would start to follow cracks in the earth down streets she had never visited, would get lost down alleyways, following a strange musk, a ringing kind of song bouncing around deep beneath her feet.

She'd miss lunch dates with Ted and then dinner dates.

I don't have time for this anymore, Ted finally said. *I have a wife and a kid*, he says. *You can't be my problem*, he says. Being sick is quite inconvenient. And that's the end of the affair.

Except for one Wednesday morning when Ted pulls Lucy into

the copier room and locks the door. They never speak. His hot brime-breath makes her head buzz and her eyes blur, while he smiles and stares at the ceiling, and through it, and up to the stars.

Six months ago, no one knew what Mr. Gardner looked like. No one ever saw him enter the office and no one ever saw him leave. If you needed to tell Mr. Gardner something, you talked to his secretary Lois. Lois hired you and fired you and negotiated with you when you wanted a raise. Lois gave you petty cash for the staff birthday parties and signed Mr. Gardner's name in the birthday card. You had to make an appointment with Lois in order to speak to Lois.

Lois had been the first from the office to go.

Lois twirled in one Wednesday morning, humming that song from the commercials and announced she was going to space.

Lois never twirled. Lois never smiled. Lois never hummed or kissed Mr. Gardner right on his bald head. She smoked cigarettes and ate powdered donuts and rolled her eyes. This was a spectacle.

The day Lois announced she was going to space was the day the office's lofty vision of Mr. Gardner was dislodged—images of him tall, handsome in a tailored suit and gelled tar black hair with a voice that rumbled with the office's collective need for a father figure.

Lois showed up on her last day in full astronaut suit, just like Ted, bearing several pink boxes of donuts and bags of her old clothes and personal items she was no longer going to need, now that she was going to live in space.

For the first time, Mr. Gardner joined the rest of the office in the little celebration around the donuts and piles of clothes and knickknacks that smelled of mothballs and heavy perfume. The father-figure-fantasy Mr. Gardner shrank some five inches, gained thirty pounds, lost a good portion of his hair, and had a voice like a squirrel being strangled.

Lucy had just gotten the earphone implant to help her focus (that day she was listening to Billie Holiday and Nina Simone) and was slipping between conversations and jazz, sipping spiked punch Lois usually only made for the office holiday party. Ted brushed by her, pausing slightly for a smell of her hair, a breath into her neck, and then rushed to Lois to ask about how she got chosen, what the was process, where did she get that great silver astronaut suit, etc.

Lois looks up at the ceiling. *Can't you hear it?* she asks. *It's like singing. It's like a chorus of stars calling out for me. My future with the Humans, out there. Can't you hear it?* Lois looks right at Lucy.

Lucy can't hear much except Billie Holiday and Lois's faraway voice.

Ted says he can hear it. Marcia and Dave hear it too. Mr. Gardner says nothing.

Lois explains that the Humans have a new Earth somewhere out in the dark. This one is sick. This one is long gone. She smiles.

At a moment during the party, when there was the most commotion and Mr. Gardner thought himself to be forgotten, Lucy saw him taking deep inhales of a pink pinstriped blouse from the Lois pile.

Lucy watches Ted as he leaves Mr. Gardner's office, still with that smile, helmet still firmly in place, his hands on his hips like a real American astronaut, like he's posing for a camera that isn't there.

Ted puts a gentle hand on Lucy's shoulder, as if she's a child who just wet the bed, and puts a brochure in her hand—spreading the good word of the Humans.

Ted mouths some words Lucy can't hear (Betty Davis is loud in her ears), but she thinks he says: *Save yourself from yourself.*

When Ted leaves, Lucy continues to draw for the rest of the afternoon. She lets the corn field spread off Mr. Gardner's window and onto the office walls, all the way to the copy room. She draws right over the dull white paint. She throws away the sharpie and pulls out thin markers and colored pencils and adds color and shade to the cornfield, to the people and the Humans within it. She draws as James Brown sings in her head, as she ignores the other echoing sounds and nods her head and closes her eyes.

When she opens them again, she has drawn long spiraling arms across the cornfield, across the people. Swirls of something dark, like that spirals in her organs or the cracks in the earth, or the smoke from the rockets heading out into space.

The first time Lucy met a Human was in the office conference room, a month after the commercials began to run, but before the TV reruns were pulled off the air. The Humans were making their way to most businesses and families and organizations, spending an hour answering questions and speaking about evacuation plans. Lucy heard very little of the conversation (she was listening to musical theatre that day – *Little Shop of Horrors*, mostly) but the image was not lost on her. Tall and impeccable, with smooth skin and finger nails long on one hand as if he was learning how to play guitar on the side, the Human hummed along through the usual speeches, and the others nodded, mesmerized, smiling. Lois set a pink box of fresh donuts in front of the Human, who took a powdered one before passing it along. As he spoke, he carefully scraped his long finger nails across the powder and brought his fingers to his lips. He managed to eat an entire donut that way, scrape by scrape.

Lucy shut off her music for a moment, letting the ring of the world fade to an annoying hum before interrupting the Human's speech.

"But how do you decide?" Lucy asked.

"How do we decide," repeated the Human.

"There's no way I would bring everyone with me. I mean, if I was starting a new colony or panning for gold or whatever the hell you all are doing."

"Whatever we're doing," repeated the Human.

"So who stays and who goes?" said Lucy.

The Human scraped his nails along the donut. The tiniest puffs of powder popped into the air. "Lucy," said the Human, "do you want to come with us."

"I'm a little busy these days," said Lucy.

The Human smiled, his teeth stretching and multiplying farther than his skull could reach. Lucy was starting to feel light headed, was feeling like she should smile back and grow out her nails and eat a donut just like that, bit by bit.

Lucy grabbed a donut and switched on her earphone again. She didn't know why she had wanted the donut, but she couldn't let it go, so there it stayed, melting into her palms until the end of the meeting.

Lucy used to make herself go to grocery stores late at night to avoid the crowd. But now shopping for frosted cereal feels like a post-apocalyptic zombie game on pause—desolate and dimly lit and smelling of spilled laundry detergent.

Before the Humans came, if Lucy was forced to visit the grocery store during a busy time, she loved to stand in the middle of the produce department, at some awkward angle, far enough into an aisle so people could only get past her by squeezing and shuffling and grumbling, and she would marvel at the brightness of the tomatoes and the smoothness of the apples, and the crispness of the lettuce. Everything seemed impossibly perfect, the colors turned up somehow, everything arranged in the way that made you feel refreshed and comforted and healthier. No ugly fruit here. So Lucy would stand there, slightly though not fully in the way, and choose the ripest reddest tomato from the stack and take a bite. The juices would shimmy down her chin and spot up her blouse, and the seeds logged along her gum line. And she would stand there and eat, waiting for someone to stop her, watching for an odd stare here, listening for a whisper there. Lucy felt as if she were suddenly solid, firmly on the earth in these moments, as if the rest of the day she were a puff of air or smoke or an odor lingering in everyone's clothes. The tomato really tasted like a tomato, and Lucy really felt like a Lucy.

One night, as Lucy stood there, eating a particularly soft vine tomato, Ted and his wife and son happened by. Ted avoided her eyes and busied himself with the avocados, checking their firmness and smell. His wife, having never been to the office, picked out a few jalapeños (which Lucy knew Ted hated). And their son smiled at Lucy, took a tomato of his own, and took a bite. Until Ted noticed and pulled his son away, swiping the tomato out of his mouth, (swooping in with a grimace and a glare at Lucy—this was before the roast beef dinner and the first commercial, but months after their first encounter in the supply closet). It was just

Lucy and the little boy, enjoying a perfect tomato in a chaotic current of shoppers.

Now, Lucy stands and waits her turn at the only check-out stand open, looking at the tabloids with pictures of celebrities waving from the doors of shuttles. She avoids the produce section and tomatoes altogether. She knows no one is taking care of the produce like they used to (the flies have increased). She knows the tomatoes are probably rotten, and there's no little boy standing there anyway, waiting to take a bite.

Lucy sort of misses people. It's a weird feeling.

A Human is waiting in line in front of Lucy one evening. The Human is buying a pack of powered donuts and nothing else. He wobbles a bit in line, his mouth hard and tight against his teeth, his silver suit tattered at the edges. The cashier quotes a price to him and the Human taps his pockets, or what would be pockets on a normal human, and makes a show of it. Lucy thinks to spot the Human a few bucks but before she can decide, the Human is already whispering something to the cashier who nods and smiles and follows the Human out of the store. The Human doesn't pay for the donuts, and the cashier is the last one in the whole store, so Lucy doesn't pay for her groceries either.

Outside, the Human is eating the donuts, white powder hanging like clouds around his face. The Human is hunched over, hungry, more like a rat in this light. His eyes are sunken, his bones protruding through cracking skin, red with rash. He meets Lucy's eyes and says something to her, but Lucy can't hear him (today it is Aimee Mann and Ani DiFranco singing in her ears).

The Human fumbles with the packaging and one of the donuts goes flying to the ground. Lucy picks it up and holds it at eye level. She can see the Human's face through the hole in the donut, perfectly framed in white powder and cake. Lucy has always liked to look at things in this way – the way that makes them seem small.

Lucy drags her nail across the edge of the donut and licks her finger. The chalky pure sugar taste reminds her of sugar cane fields in Hawaii, where her mother and father took her years ago, when she was too young to appreciate the absence of cracks in the earth, the feeling that everything and everyone was okay, just for a moment. She realizes that she has been drawing sugar cane and not corn. She has driven past a cornfield or two. But she has walked through sugar cane beneath an impossibly blue sky.

The hungry Human drags a nail along the other side of the donut and licks it off. He still does not smile.

A second Human appears from behind them, yanking the hungry Human away toward a small, silver vessel parked in an accessible parking spot.

The cashier smiles and runs after them, waiting to be rescued.

Lucy keeps drawing, all the way to the supply closet, through cubicles one through her own cubicle twenty-nine—she draws right onto the walls and floors, using post-it notes and scrap paper to cover the rougher surfaces. The cornfield grows longer and taller and more detailed, morphing into a sugar cane field from Lucy's memory, the spiral arms reaching out farther and farther, twisting through the roots of the imaginary field.

She stops when she finishes a drawing of herself and Mr. Gardner, sitting on a bench, surrounded by the tallest of the tall sugar cane, looking up into the sky, nothing hovering above them, nothing pulling them into a spaceship.

She doesn't know what should happen next. She looks down at

the floor and notices a crack for the first time, a crack just like the ones in the earth, all the way up on the tenth floor.

Lucy switches off her earphones. A gurgling of sounds fills her ears. A tiny moan reverberates from the crack in the floor.

Mr. Gardner says something Lucy can't quite hear, pats her shoulder, and walks back to his office.

Lucy asks Mr. Gardner to repeat what he said. *Please repeat it.*

Outside, a little too close to their office, a rocket ship launches into the sky, and for a moment Lucy and Mr. Gardner are drowning in the rumbling, their words lost between a screeching of earth and sky.

Vó Úrsula's Magical Shop for Soul-Aches

Victoria V.

Victoria is a Brazilian who sometimes reads and sometimes writes, but has always been passionate about all kinds of stories. When she's not dealing with her never ending to-read pile or adopting new succulents and cacti, she lives her secret life as an average young adult trying to figure out how the world works. You may find her in one of her hometown's dusty second-hand bookshops or, once in a while, on her corner of the internet.

Everything is the tip of a mystery.

João Guimarães Rosa

No one could deny that the yellow house, number 107, looked a bit odd. Funny, even.

An unobservant passer-by would easily attribute it to the light paint that peeled off the walls, or to the tacky curtains that hung out of the windows. But, after a close look, one could swear the colorful flowers on the balcony bent towards each other in a way that made them seem to be politely chatting all day long.

Most people would forget these details right after noticing them: it could be just another of the old, dusty thrift shops downtown. To the few of them who decided to go in, that funny house soon became unmistakable. After all, the city didn't have any other stores that sold cures for every imaginable soul-ache, carefully bottled in crystalline glass.

To Berenice and Benjamin dos Santos, however, it was home.

Time passed in different ways inside Vó Úrsula's house. Downstairs, in the store, the hours flew by even when there were no customers. Upstairs, where Benjamin lived with his cousin and his grandmother, the minutes seemed to flow as the cool and calm diaphanous waters of a river.

What intrigued him the most, though, was how time worked in the tight, cozy room in the attic, that he and Berenice had nick-named The Nook. It went by quickly when it needed to, but it also could freeze the clock hands at the right split second and make a pleasant afternoon feel eternal.

He had questioned his grandmother about it, once, and her only reply had been a smile.

Benjamin hit his head on the wall with a startle when Berenice snapped her fingers in front of his face.

"Hey!"

"Earth calling." Berenice laughed at her own robotic voice. Despite his best efforts to look annoyed, he couldn't suppress a grin. "A penny for your thoughts, sir? I won't take 'no' as an answer," she said. Benjamin giggled, dodging her tickling fingers.

"It's nothing." He pointed his chin towards her notebook, left open on the armrest. "What are you doing this time?"

"Oh, I'm glad you asked." She tossed it to him, her eyes beaming as she explained. "It's a comic for the university's free press, you see. It's about this captain from the Army who really wants to be a politician, but he's dumb and clumsy and no one ever listens to him. One day, he wakes up to find out that he's the President, and he has to pretend he knows what he's doing, so no one finds out he's actually a fraud."

"What happens at the end?"

"I'm still deciding." She shrugged and grabbed the notebook from his lap. "Ah, what is it? You're making that face again."

"What face?"

"The *thinking Benjamin* face." Berenice crossed her legs and stretched her back. "Don't look at me like that; it was your friend who came up with it."

"What friend?"

"Eustácio, of course. Who else would it be? He comes here more often than our own cat."

"Uh, I..." Benjamin stuttered, feeling the blood flush to his face. "You..."

"I don't mind, though. He's always polite, and I like him, if you want my opinion." She turned her head over her shoulder and glanced at the old clock on the wall. The store was about to close, and it was almost time for them to go downstairs and help Vó Úrsula organize it. "Have you got any plans for tonight?"

"It's Wednesday evening, Berenice. Unless you consider studying geometry as plans...no, I don't." He jumped out of the bed onto the carpet on the floor that was, somehow, always warm. "The students' union is meeting here tonight, isn't it?"

"The *free* students' union," she corrected, and followed him down the spiral staircase.

"Does Grandma know?"

Berenice stopped at the top of the second staircase, hands on her hips. "What, that we're having a meeting here?"

"No, of course she knows that. I'm talking about you writing for the free press."

"Well, she hasn't asked for the details of what we do at the meetings. And it's not like it's risky or anything. I'm just going to give it to Clarice, and she'll pass it to her boyfriend, who helps to organize the papers. He just has to slip it in, nothing more." She smiled at him, reassuring. "We don't do dangerous, illegal things. You know, we're not the MR-8." Berenice snorted. "We're just... students who like to think freely and critically. And I still insist that you should join us, at least once."

Benjamin sighed. "You know my father doesn't like me getting involved with these...things."

"First, Uncle Michel is almost 400 kilometers away from here; he'll never know. Second, nothing bad will happen inside this house. Vó Úrsula's word."

"I know," he murmured.

A black cat came running upstairs and rubbed his fur against Benjamin's heels.

"Hello, Ernesto!" he said, smiling, as he picked him up.

"So is this how you thank me for getting you out of the streets?" Berenice spoke to the animal, pretending to be annoyed while she caressed the back of his ears.

"It's fair that he likes me more. I nearly broke my arm climbing that tree!"

"Stop being so dramatic! It was just a scratch."

"A scratch that made me wear a splint for two weeks, you say?"

Berenice elbowed him and he laughed.

The staircase led to the dusty back of the store. Around them, bottles filled with colorful liquids were displayed on shelves made of dark wood that had been meticulously organized according to a logic only Vó Úrsula could understand. In the first weeks after Benjamin had moved to live with his grandmother, he would often get lost among them, as if there were an insurmountable maze between the shop and the house. Now, almost three years later, he was almost sure that the racks made way for him to pass.

He had also asked Vó Úrsula about that. And, as always, she had only smiled.

"There you are! Right on time!" Úrsula said from behind the counter. Her skin, the same deep shade of mahogany that her grandchildren had inherited from her, was bathed in the dim golden light from the lamp on the ceiling. "Your friend has just arrived, dear."

Eustácio, leaning against the wall, gave Benjamin a shy smile when their eyes met. "Hi. Uh, I'm sorry about coming without warning, but..."

"Son, you know you'll always be welcome here," Vó Úrsula interrupted with a wide smile. "Berenice, my dear, will you help me over there? There are some new flasks I must label."

"Of course, Grandma. It's nice to see you, Eustácio." She winked at him as she followed Vó Úrsula inside the store.

"Is everything all right?" Benjamin asked when they finally were left alone, after a long silence. Ernesto jumped to the floor with one fluid movement and meowed at the boys before escaping to the street.

"Yes. Yes, you don't have to worry."

He quickly understood. It wasn't the first time that Eustácio had knocked at his door on a random evening, and it wasn't the first time Benjamin couldn't help but worry. It had taken him a while (and some straightforward hints from Berenice) to realize that his friend longed for space instead of advice, and that his simply being there was more than enough.

"Let's go upstairs, so I'll beat you at chess."

"Not happening, Benjamin. I've been training." His eyes glittered, and he smiled for the first time since he had arrived.

"Checkmate," Benjamin said with a victorious smile, and finger-flicked the white king.

Eustácio sighed, exasperated, and covered his face with his hands. "You are unbelievable."

He laughed and supressed a yawn. "Another round?"

"I propose a ten-minute truce," Eustácio suggested, with his typical sideways smile. He glanced at the clock on the wall that patiently kept track of the flowing time. "Oh, I didn't notice it was so late. I...should go."

It was past midnight. The Nook was quiet, except for the loud voices of the students rising from the kitchen.

"It's too late, Eustácio. It's..." He interrupted himself before he could say *dangerous*. The stories about the police patrols that roamed the empty streets were known by all. The government had promised to fight crime, but much of the violence and fear that haunted the cities came from the so-called law enforcement, as well. "Do your aunt and uncle know you're here?"

"Not really. They're not home tonight, and I don't think my cousins noticed when I left." He took off his glasses and wiped the round lenses on his shirt. "We've got school tomorrow, anyway."

"I've got a spare uniform, and I could lend you a notebook," Benjamin said without thinking twice. Eustácio put his glasses back on and stared at him in silence. "Hm, it wouldn't be a problem for me, and you wouldn't have to go back alone."

"Are you sure?" he asked in a quiet voice. "Won't your grandmother mind?"

"Not even a little bit. The whole student union is downstairs, and they're way noisier than you are. Everyone is always welcome," Benjamin explained, while organizing the chess pieces inside the cardboard box, "as long as we clean up the mess we make."

"Well, then...thank you." Eustácio's smile faded when loud, amused laughs came from downstairs. He let his gaze drift out of the small window, into the dark, moonless night, and bit his inner lip. "Your cousin and her friends remind me of so much my parents," he said suddenly. "Their friends used to meet at our old house, and...and they were all so hopeful. They were sure that it would all end in a couple of years. And here we are."

"None of this will last forever." Benjamin was unsure if he believed his own words.

"It already feels like forever," he murmured. "I miss them."

"I'm sure they are all right, just waiting until it's over so they can come back to you." As soon as the words came to life, Benjamin remembered Vó Úrsulas advice about how a thin line separated hope from foolishness. He looked down to fidget with his fingers.

"Are you being kind or honest?" asked Eustácio gently, seeing through his embarrassment.

"A little bit of both," he admitted.

"A little bit of both will do, I guess."

Something inside Benjamin melted when Eustácio gave him a half-hearted smile and ran his fingers through his messy, curly hair. A quiet, cool darkness embraced the room when he turned off the lights, and, laying on the bed, he could only see the dim skyline of the city.

On the couch, Eustácio turned around under his sheets.

"Hey, Benjamin?"

"Yeah?" He could hear his own heart beating in the fragile quiet that had surrounded them.

"It's...it's nothing. Good night."

"Good night."

It was another hot, muggy day in the middle of winter. An invisible cloud of heat seemed to have overtaken the streets, and Benjamin's shirt was wet with sweat under his heavy backpack. He stood for a moment on the threshold, enjoying the breath of fresh air that caressed his cheeks.

"Hello, Grandma!"

He frowned when his voice got lost in the empty hall.

"Berenice? Grandma?" he called again, and swallowed hard when no answer came. He locked the door and rubbed his sweaty palms against each other, turning to the store.

The simple decorations and the bottles were where Vó Úrsula had left them. Except for a sinking feeling in his chest, everything was where it should be. He searched the counter for one of the notes she used to write when she had to leave unexpectedly, and was about to go outside and ask their neighbors if they had seen something strange when Ernesto came from behind one of the racks. He meowed at the boy before turning around and heading upstairs. Half relieved, half resigned, Benjamin followed his cat.

As he reached the final steps, the soft buzz of polite talk grew louder. Ernesto stopped, looked at him for a long second, then turned around and went back downstairs. Benjamin shook his head and allowed himself to smile.

Vó Úrsula sat at the kitchen table, in front of a thin girl who could have been made of porcelain and whose muddy green eyes got wider when she saw him. She wasn't unfamiliar, but he couldn't remind where he'd seen her before.

"Benjamin, my dear, please don't mind us," said Vó Úrsula without turning to face him.

"Of...of course. Excuse me." He smiled at the girl before heading to the attic, but she looked away. The voices only echoed again when he was too far away tounderstand the conversation.

He slammed the Nook's door behind him, took off his shoes, and let his backpack fall on the floor. He jumped back when he caught a glimpse of Berenice, who laid on the sofa as she scribbled on her notebook.

"Oh, hey, you," she said, barely lifting her eyes from her work.

"I didn't know you'd be here this early." He picked up one of the colorful cushions with a crochet pillow cover and sat by her side. "You and Grandma scared me. The shop was empty when I arrived. I thought...something might have happened to you."

"Well, no. At least not yet."

"What do you mean?"

"Our editor-in-chief and a journalist are missing, so we're all on leave until our bosses decide what to do. It had something to do with the new retroactive censorship decree." Berenice straightened her back and put her notebook on the floor. "And the police found Clarice's boyfriend distributing the leaflets at the university, and he only came back two days later. He won't even leave his bed." She shook her head and opened her mouth to say something, but gave up.

"Vó Úrsula said we're safe here, remember?" he suggested, unsure.

"Hiding here in safety isn't worth anything when the whole world is falling apart. We must stop pretending everything is all right."

"I wasn't..."

"I know." She ran her hands over her face, and Benjamin pretended to not see her eyes welling up with tears she rubbed away. "I'm sorry."

"Hey, it's nothing." He gave her a friendly squeeze on the knee, and she forced a smile. "Promise me you'll stay safe." She faced him, her eyes a reflection of Vó Úrsula's. "Please. I can't afford to lose you."

"I'll do my best, but promise you'll do your best, too."

"I do." He rose his pinky. Berenice rolled her eyes and intertwined her finger with his. "Listen, did you already tell Grandma about it? I'm sure she may have one or two things to help."

"I'm not sure if *simpatias* are efficient against guns, Ben. But no, not yet. It was odd, she wasn't home when I arrived, and she didn't leave a note. Have you seen her?"

"She was at the kitchen with a red-haired girl."

"The one who's always around?"

He frowned. "Yes, that one. I was trying to remember where I knew her from."

Berenice crossed her legs and picked up her notebook from the floor. "Don't you think she's too young to come to a store that sells cures for soul-aches? I wouldn't say she's thirteen."

"Maybe." He shrugged. "Or maybe the world is upside-down and we haven't noticed."

"We'll fix it, then. We have no other choice but to fix it."

Benjamin smiled at her, telling himself to believe her words were true.

As on all Friday evenings, the shop was quiet. The crystalline silences that hid between the shelves and under the carpets crawled out as soon as Vó Úrsula and Berenice vanished into the street, and the house soon became so still it was possible to hear polite murmurs coming from the flowers on the balcony.

Benjamin didn't mind the emptiness, though, especially when Eustácio was there to fill it.

He entered his bedroom balancing a bottle of lemonade in one hand and a jar of cookies in the other, and sat on the wooden floor. Eating at the Nook was one of the few strict prohibitions Vó Úrsula had determined, so the boys had non-verbally agreed to snack in Benjamin's narrow room, equipped with an old desk and a bed.

He passed the jar to Eustácio, who seemed hesitant to accept it.

"Did you make these?" he asked after finally taking a small bite.

"Oh, no. It was one of Grandma's clients who baked them for us, that's why they're this tasty." Benjamin shoved another biscuit into his mouth at once. "He had backaches that would never go away, no matter what he did. Grandma said it turned out his soul was hurting so much that the pain began to affect his body. He brought us this to thank her," he explained, and tapped the metallic lid with the tips of his fingers.

"May I ask you something?" said Eustácio quietly.

"Sure."

"How do the cures for soul-aches work? I've always wanted to ask you that, but..." he shook his head. "I never knew when."

"I guess I'll disappoint you, because I actually don't know." Eustácio refused the last cookie. Benjamin took it and put the jar aside. "It must have something to do with magic, though."

"Magic?" He sounded incredulous.

"Why not?"

"Oh, it's...I just didn't know you were the kind of person who believed in it."

"It depends on what you call magic. I definitely don't believe in witches who live in haunted castles and brew bubbling potions." He looked around the room, the first place that had felt truly his and that, somehow, was always cozier than the one on his parents' house. "But, when you look at the world, at life...there are always these tiny details no one can explain. Mysteries." He smiled at Eustácio, whose cheeks turned a light, almost unnoticeable shade of red. "Some people call them miracles. I prefer to see it as magic."

"I never thought of it that way."

"Living with Vó Úrsula and with Berenice teaches you something about things you can't explain. Just like...just like when Berenice decided to bring Ernesto home. There are thousands of stray cats out there, and it was him that she always saw on her way to the university, and it was him who climbed the tree that day when we were coming back home." He grinned when the memory of that cloudy afternoon came to his mind. "Ernesto is the strangest cat I've ever seen, and somehow he fits into this place as if he'd always belonged here. Also, I didn't break any bones when I fell from the tree, which is another great miracle. Or...let's see..."

"When you're late for your first day at school, and the only seat available is behind a person who ends up becoming, uh..."

"A part of your life that has always seemed to be there," completed Benjamin, without thinking.

"Yes, a part of your life that has always seemed to be there." Eustácio came a little closer, and all Benjamin could see were his big, dark hazel eyes that seemed to embrace the entire universe behind the round lenses. "You are one of the best little mysteries in my life, Benjamin," he said in a soft whisper.

Time stopped. Benjamin leant forward and kissed him.

When they pulled away a split second later, his racing heart was about to come out of his chest. Eustácio's cheeks were flushed, but he didn't look away.

"I'm...I'm sorry, I...Are you sure you..."

Eustácio interrupted him by pulling him closer, into a longer kiss.

Unable to look away from each other's eyes, the boys stayed silent, breathing slowly, as if any sound could break the unending ephemerality of that moment. Eustácio's fingertips ran down Benjamin's cheek.

"It's you. It's always been you," Benjamin said.

"It's always been you, too," Eustácio murmured.

Another eternity passed inside a single second. They giggled as children who had just begun to discover the world.

Eustácio grabbed Benjamin's hand and held him back. "Are you sure your grandmother won't mind it?"

"Hey. Relax." He squeezed Eustácio's hand and smiled, leading him downstairs. "I'm just going to show you the store."

Eustácio's laugh filled the empty house. Vó Úrsula had set off to see a friend without warning, so the store had been closed earlier on that drizzly Monday night, leaving the two boys alone, to their delight.

Everything had seemed to fall into place in the past few weeks. Berenice looked satisfied every morning before going to her new-found job. Eustácio's visits to the house had become longer and more frequent. It could be the proximity of the mid-year vacations, but the bad news didn't come as frequently as it did before, and Benjamin found himself smiling more often.

He stood on the tip of his toes and reached for one of the round bottles on the racks, filled with a burbling rose-colored liquid, that shimmered when bathed by sunlight. "For melancholy and dismay caused by the sudden awareness of the state of the world," he read from the note attached to the cork. "Use in moderation."

He passed it to Eustácio, who held the bottle with the caution of someone handling a precious gem. "It's...beautiful. Strange, but beautiful." He handed it back with a smile and looked over the other bottles on the shelf. "Bottled hope. It must be a best-seller these days," he added.

"Well, Grandma is the one who prescribes it, but once she told me that most people go to her because of heartbreaks, and then end up figuring out that their souls were hurting more than they first thought," Benjamin explained while putting the flask back in its original place. A rich yellow liquid that swirled inside the bottle caught his attention. "Here, take a look at this one. 'Homesickness, longing: *saudades* in general. Be careful when...' Ernesto, what are you up to?"

The cat turned to them and meowed. He ran to the back of the store, where he began to scratch the wall.

"Oh, Ernesto, please!" he complained.

Before Benjamin could stop him, the loud noise of a car parking came from outside, quickly followed by impatient knocks on the door.

Eustácio frowned at him. "I didn't know your family had a car."

"We don't."

They exchanged a meaningful look as color slowly vanished from Eustácio's face. Ernesto meowed again, and the thumps became quicker and stronger.

"Come on," whispered Benjamin, and he took his cold hand. They hurried to the back of the store as silently as they could, where Ernesto, rather annoyed, pawed the wall. It took Benjamin a few precious seconds to notice it was, in fact, a hidden door. He traced its shape with the tips of his fingers and made it open with a click.

"What is this?"

"I'm not sure. I guess it's..." He peeked inside, but couldn't see what was before his own nose. A soft perfume of rue and rosemary that resembled the one Vó Úrsula herself always used came out of the room, and Benjamin suddenly understood. "It must be the stock."

Ernesto purred and slipped into the room.

"Are we supposed to be here?" Eustácio asked. His voice trailed off when indistinguishable voices began to shout outside. Benjamin could distinguish Vó Úrsula's usually calm tone rising above the others.

"It let us find it."

Ernesto meowed again. Outside, a key turned around in the lock one, two, three times. Still holding hands, the boys walked into the unknown, and the thin door closed behind them before the furious steps could storm the store.

Benjamin fumbled around in the dark until he could touch a wall, and helped Eustácio sit down against it. The sweet smell that invaded his lungs when he took a deep breath brought a strange sense of calm, as if he were on a safe shore watching a stormy sea.

"All I'm asking you to do is to be reasonable." Vó Úrsula's voice echoed, somewhere between calm and stern. "Honestly, Sérgio, I didn't expect you to believe the tittle-tattle."

"Tittle-tattle?" The man snorted. "Would you prefer to testify at the police station instead, Úrsula?"

"Testify about what? Witchcraft?" It was Vó Úrsula's turn to laugh. "Flouting morality and good behavior?"

"Captain Braga..."

Eustácio gasped when the second man spoke. Benjamin drew closer to him. "What's it?" he asked, on a murmur.

"My uncle," was the faint answer. "It's his voice."

"Are you sure?"

As if to confirm it, Sérgio spoke again. "...Mr. Lisboa is a model citizen, and I have my own reasons to trust him. Úrsula, I know that you and I have our differences, but everything will be easier if you cooperate. Don't make me call the police."

This time, Vó Úrsula didn't speak. Benjamin noticed Eustácio was shaking. *It's all right*, he wanted to say, but the words wouldn't leave his mouth.

"What the hell is this place?" mocked Mr. Lisboa, who appeared to be pacing around.

"It might not look as much, sir, but this is how I sustain my family. How can I help you today?" she asked in her most courteous voice.

"What do you want with my nephew?" he said, dry.

A shiver went down Benjamin's spine and he closed his eyes, despite the darkness. By his side, Eustácio struggled against his own short breaths.

"Eustácio?" he called, but received no answer.

"I'm sorry?" said Vó Úrsula, after a quiet moment.

"The boy keeps slipping out to come here and thinks that I don't notice. He's up to something, just like his parents were," he grunted.

"With all due respect, Mr. Braga, this is my store, and not the

Communist Party headquarters. People come to me for different reasons, and I'm sure your nephew has his." She sighed. "May I help you with something else?"

"I could call some of my men for you, Mr. Lisboa," suggested Sérgio, breaking the silence.

Mr. Lisboa clicked his tongue. "I don't think it will be necessary, Captain. I've seen enough." His footsteps went back and forth, an angry animal walking in circles. "If the boy mysteriously pops around here anytime, Úrsula, kindly tell him that he doesn't need to come back home. Cibele and I already know that he..." He held back. "Anyway. Take care, ma'am."

"Can I help you with something else, Sérgio?"

He whispered something to her. The footsteps went away before Vó Úrsula could reply. When the door slammed with a loud blow, thunder boomed outside, and Benjamin could swear that the rain suddenly became heavier.

He put his hand on Eustácio's shoulder.

"Please, don't say anything," Eustácio mumbled, and dissolved into silent tears.

A click echoed across the dark room, and a soft brush of light illuminated the dusty shelves when Vó Úrsula's silhouette appeared in the door.

"Oh, my children," was all that she said, but it was enough for Benjamin's eyes to fill up with water.

"You," said Berenice, resting her cup of tea on her crossed legs, "have got that look on your face. Again."

"It's nothing," replied Benjamin, barely raising his eyes from his textbook. Between them, on the kitchen table, her latest disastrous attempt at baking a cake waited, untouched.

"It's been 'nothing' for the past weeks, eh?"

"I'm just tired."

She rested her chin on her hand and squinted at him. "Is it because of your friend?"

"No. I mean, that too." The sentences in the physics textbook made less sense than they usually did. He closed it and shook his head, defeated. "I'm not even sure about what we are anymore. We haven't talked since...*that* happened, and he hasn't gone to school these last few days. Eustácio never skips class, Berenice."

"He might just be sick."

"You know what I'm talking about." He sighed and added in a lower voice, "You know what happens out there."

She looked down. "I do."

They had heard the stories about people who vanished in the middle of the night and never came back the same, about far-off places where the unimaginable happened.

"And you know there's nothing I can do about it," he added.

"I do." Berenice smiled sadly, and tapped her fingertips on the table. "Sometimes all we can do is give time to time, Ben, and hope that things will work out."

"What if there isn't enough time?"

"Then we pray for one of life's miracles to happen. Or," she said, her eyes sparkling, "you could just go across the street and ask the lady who *brings back your lost love in seven days* for help."

"Eustácio is not my lost love, Berenice!"

She rose her eyebrows and leant back on her chair. "I never told you because I thought it would make you feel awkward, but I always found that you two looked rather cute together."

"You're making it awkward now."

"It was my intention."

Before he could think of a reply, the strident doorbell rang. He frowned at Berenice.

"It must be the salesman," she said, reading his thoughts. He followed her downstairs, where neither Vó Úrsula nor Ernesto were anywhere to be seen.

"Where is Grandma?"

"Taking her evening nap, I guess." Berenice was searching for the keys in the counter's drawers when the bell sounded again. "I'm coming!" she yelled.

He waited besides her, cracking his knuckles. She unlocked the door, and his disappointment faded into astonishment when the red-haired girl, holding their cat in her arms, shyly stepped inside.

"I...I found him near my garden," she explained, and handed him to Berenice. "I...he seemed to be lost."

"Oh. Thank you." Ernesto meowed, and she petted his head before putting him on the ground. "He likes to walk around the neighborhood, so you don't have to worry if you see him wandering."

"Is your grandmother home?" the girl asked bluntly. She wound and unwound her fingers in her white blouse.

Berenice glanced at her cousin.

"The store is closed," he intervened. "Uh, maybe you should come back tomorrow morning."

"I'll be really quick, I promise."

"Listen, hm...what's your name?" Berenice asked.

"Clara."

"Listen, Clara, she was sleeping, and she hates it when we wake her up," Berenice explained with an unusual patience. "Maybe we could help you. Right, Ben?"

"Right," he nodded, and tried to smile at the girl.

"I don't think you really can." Benjamin and Berenice exchanged another look. "I'm sorry, but I..."

"Ah, there you are!" interrupted Vó Úrsula. Her long red dress dragged on the ground behind her, hiding her bare feet. "It's nice to see you again, Clara, dear."

"Ma'am, I heard about what happened, and when I found your cat in my garden, I knew I had to come." She stumbled on her words and walked past the two cousins.

"You don't need to call me that, dear. And...you may talk to me here," she said, looking at Benjamin and Berenice. "I don't mind if my grandchildren listen."

Clara looked back before continuing, unsure. "I know that my father...my father was here. He discovered that you've been teaching me, and he was furious." She took a shaky breath. "He told me I can never come back because you work for the Devil, but I know it's not true...is it?"

"There is no Devil, Clara. Only us. Only people." Vó Úrsula's words hovered above their heads in the seconds that followed.

"I'm so sorry. I shouldn't have told him when he asked me, but...I was so scared. It was my fault, I'm sorry." The girl shook her head. "I'll understand if you can't teach me anymore, I..."

"Oh, dear." Vó Úrsula put her hand on Clara's fragile shoulder and gave her a warm smile. "If I can teach you something more important than how to cure people's souls, it's that we should never let each other go, especially in times of need. You'll always be welcome here."

"Are...are you sure?"

"Of course. Now...your mother must be waiting for you. Go, but come back tomorrow at the usual time."

Beaming, the girl relaxed her shoulders, as if her body had suddenly become lighter. "Oh, thank you. Thank you!"

"Stay safe, Eleonora," warned Vó Úrsula. "Take care."

"I will. Until tomorrow, Vó Úrsula!"

As fast as she had arrived, she turned around and left through the open door, not bothering to close it behind her. A fluttering veil of silence fell upon the store.

Úrsula turned around and sat behind the counter. Benjamin glanced at Berenice, who kept her eyes low.

"I should have told you two earlier," Úrsula finally said, and placed her wrinkled hands on the table.

"Who is her father?" he asked at once.

Vó Úrsula shook her head and sighed. "Oh, Benjamin. Sérgio...

Sérgio is not a stranger to me. Before you two came to live with me, even before the *coup*, we used to be friends. I'd spend the most pleasant evenings with him and little Clara." She smiled, dwelling on memories. "But '64 happened and he changed into a man I no longer recognize. He must have been around when Eustácio's uncle came looking for him. An ugly coincidence."

"An ugly coincidence?" He felt his voice raise.

"Ben!..." Berenice reprimanded.

"What if you hadn't arrived in time? What if Mr. Lisboa had decided to call the police, or denounce us? You know what they do to people like me, to people like Berenice, and even to people like you, Grandma! What does this man know and why is the girl so important to you?"

"You wouldn't understand."

"Well, I definitely don't!" he said, ignoring Berenice's burning gaze. "I definitely don't," he repeated, his voice trailing off.

Vó Úrsula stood up, put her hands on the table, and looked around.

"Clara has eyes that can look into people's souls, and hands that can soothe and heal them," she explained. "Her father thinks it's witchcraft, but it's a gift. And just like my godmother taught me how to use my talents for the greater good, it's now my time to pass it on." She turned to her grandchildren, her honey-colored eyes sparkling in the shadows like one of the glittering flasks around them. "I'm getting older and older, and the world is still hurting. I now see that when I was busy looking outside, I forgot that my most precious things are here, inside my own family. You two know that I love you, unconditionally, and that I shall do everything within my reach to keep you safe. So I hope you'll forgive me, but I also hope you'll understand why I do what I do."

Benjamin opened his mouth to speak, but all that came out was a shy, short sob, quickly followed by others. Before his brain could begin to work again, Berenice threw her arms around him, and Vó Úrsula came from behind the counter to embrace them both.

He closed his eyes and let the perfume of rue and rosemary take him to a quiet place where love and happiness would always be proven true.

Ernesto jumped from Benjamin's lap even before the doorbell echoed across the empty house.

It was another Friday night, and Vó Úrsula and Berenice had already set off for their night-time excursions. Benjamin carefully placed his book on his bed, next to the steaming cup of tea, and went downstairs, jumping the last few steps, with Ernesto at his heels.

Outside, the heavy rain tapped on the windows in a surprisingly peaceful harmony. The calmness that had spread inside him faded when he unlocked the door to find Eustácio, holding a suitcase and soaked from head to toe, standing on the threshold.

"I have nowhere to go. I..."

Benjamin made him enter the store and pulled him into a long hug. Trembling, Eustácio dropped his suitcase on the floor and hugged him back.

"Heavens, I was worried about you," he said.

"And I was awful to you," Eustácio mumbled. "I'm sorry."

"Hey, everything's fine now," Benjamin reassured him, and smiled at him when they broke apart. "It really is. Listen, what happened? Did they tell you to leave? Are you all right?"

"Not...really," he answered, perhaps all questions at once, and took off his glasses to rub his eyes. "I'm sorry, I don't even know what to say."

"Then say nothing,'" he said gently, and headed to the stairs. "Come on, let's find you some dry clothes and I'll make you something warm to drink."

Eustácio, however, didn't move.

"What's the matter?" Benjamin asked, turning back to him.

"It's..." He took a deep breath and looked around. "Won't your grandmother mind?"

"For heaven's sake." Something warm spread inside his chest, and he smiled when Ernesto walked around Eustácio's feet, purring. The house bid him welcome. "You're home."

A gentle breeze came from outside. Benjamin, still waiting for sleepiness to come, stared at the full moon spreading its light on the dark, cloudy sky. Ernesto had curled up on the Nook's parapet, and he was not sure whether the cat was asleep or just observing the empty street.

Eustácio, who was laying on the sofa, took another short breath and turned around under his sheets.

"Hey," Benjamin called. "Can't sleep?"

"Not at all."

"Nightmares?"

"That too," he murmured.

In the darkness, Benjamin reached for the light switch, and the single lamp shed its weak yellowish light upon the room.

"Don't worry about me; I'm fine."

"Are you sure?"

"No," he admitted after a short pause, and laughed, humorless. "Would you mind if I, hm, stayed there with you for a little?" he asked, suddenly serious, in a shy murmur.

"Of course not."

The bed felt wider as they tried to settle down. Benjamin turned off the lights and a comforting darkness fell upon the Nook as the two boys lay, in silence, side by side.

"They wanted to admit me to a clinic," Eustácio said suddenly. "My uncle was fuming when I got home. Later he found out I'd overheard him talking to a preacher on the phone, so he wouldn't let me go to class because he thought I'd run away or hide. That's more or less what happened. I should have told you earlier."

"Hey, it's ok," he managed to say, despite the growing lump in his throat. "You're safe now and everything's going to be fine. You'll see."

"I'm not sure, I..." He sighed and moved towards the edge of the mattress. "I don't know where to go. I have no idea what to do next. I guess I never did, since Mom and Dad disappeared."

"What do you mean?"

"I must find somewhere to live. I can't stay here forever...can I?"

"Well, it doesn't have to be forever, but I'm sure Berenice and Vó Úrsula wouldn't mind if you stuck with us for as long as you need to. It's home, remember?" Eustácio didn't answer, but he turned his head on the pillow to look at him. "And...if us being whatever we are will make it weird or uncomfortable, then we can just be friends again, as we always were." The words felt heavy and his stomach sank, but he smiled. "You're still my best friend, after all."

"Are you sure?" Eustácio said, almost voiceless.

"Absolutely."

Benjamin closed his eyes and inhaled the fresh air that came in through the window. The night smelled of a profound silence. He startled when Eustácio's cold hand reached for his.

"Whatever we are, Ben...I like it. I like the idea of us."

"It's not a bad idea, when you stop to think about it."

"No, it's definitely not."

Trying not to burst into relieved giggles, they pulled each other closer. Breathing had never felt so easy, and, caught in the middle of that ephemeral eternity, Benjamin let himself drift into sleep.

The next morning, when the first beams of sunlight woke them up, their fingers were still intertwined.

To most people, it was still the same old yellow house. An attentive passer-by could tell that something had changed on its facade, despite not being able to pinpoint exactly where. Maybe it was the curtains on the windows that seemed to glitter. Maybe it was the front door that seemed to smile, inviting. Or maybe it was the black cat that sometimes stood by the porch, and whose green eyes seemed to peek inside people's souls.

The ones who dared to go in would find Vó Úrsula standing by the counter, and often a girl with hair as red as flames would be by her side. Sometimes, a kind, short young woman with fire in her eyes would pass by. Sometimes, a young man who had her same eyes would serve the customers tea, helped by another boy who didn't speak much and whose hair was always messy.

On some nights, finely-tuned ears could hear voices full of hope coming out of the windows. On others, the neighborhood was more silent than usual, and the sharpest eyes could spot two figures at the attic's small window. Most times, they would just stand together and look at the world outside.

It was, indeed, an odd house. Funny, even.

To Berenice, Benjamin, and Eustácio, however, it was home. And it would still be for the many years to come.

The Family Recipe

Alexandra Grunberg

Alexandra Grunberg is a Glasgow-based author, poet, and screenwriter. Her short stories have appeared in various online magazines including Daily Science Fiction, Fantastic Stories of the Imagination, and Flash Fiction Online. She is the resident screenwriter for the film production company Magic Dog Productions.

It was never just a cookbook.

That was what Rosalie Pennington told her daughter, Martha, when she handed her the heavy book wrapped in plain brown paper, tied with rough twine. It was also a cookbook; and there were recipes for various meals organized from appetizers to desserts. But it was made by someone very special, someone who offered these gifts to the family long ago, though Rosalie was the first to bind each gift together in one thick hardcover book. She wrote her name carefully in the top left corner of the book: one inch down, one inch in. For such a precise woman, Martha thought each recipe would perfectly match the index. But every so often, in between the ingredients and instructions, she would find a different type of recipe calling for herbs not found in every person's garden. The whisking gave way to grinding with a mortar and pestle and instead of a Crock-Pot she had to pull out her cauldron. Martha eventually spilled hollandaise sauce over a love spell, but by then she was Martha Carraway. She had no need for wooing anymore and did not see it as much of a loss compared with everything she had gained.

Martha could not fully remove the stain by the time she wrapped the book in old magazines and red ribbon and handed it down to her daughter, Beverley. Beverley learned to make Yorkshire puddings that cheered every roast dinner and poppets that guarded against every curse in the same evening. Years later, when she was making pancakes with her children, two pages were merged together for all eternity through the binding powers of maple syrup. Beverly never knew what spells were lost, but she did not miss them as much as she enjoyed being chased by her children who threatened her with maple-coated palms and plastered her with sticky handprints. And her son, Peter, did not ask what was missing on the day he tore off the festive Christmas wrapping paper. He was just pleased to have that pancake recipe again.

Peter did make a few of the charms that he found inserted in the midst of recipes for savory jellies. When one of his concoctions bubbled over, improvisation turning to a sour mess, the pages for the jellies were lost along with the charms. Peter regretted the loss of the charms much more than the loss of the jellies, but he penned in as many of the instructions as he could remember on the margins surrounding the introduction to tea sandwiches. He soon realized that the recipes for the tea-infused cocktails did not have alcoholic special ingredients. He learned the next summer, though, that the ingredients were just as flammable as alcohol. But he had been preparing enough picnics with his daughter, Evelyn, that she was able to list some of the lost recipes on the back of a page for crème brûlée. And she had improvised enough with her father to add a few new recipes of her own.

By the time Evelyn passed the book down to her son, Nathaniel, and he passed it down to his niece Millie, and she passed it down to her granddaughter Rosalie, there was little left of that original cookbook wrapped so carefully in brown paper by the original Rosalie besides her curvy signature inked on the inside of the front cover. The newest Rosalie added her name to the end of the list: following several other Rosalies, a few Peters, two or three Marthas, and the smudged pawprint of a cat lovingly named Pancake. The newest Rosalie also added in a few recipes of her own, ones that replaced the correct merging of candle wax with the correct mashup of mp3s. Her potions could be made just as easily in the microwave as in a cauldron. And her recipe for pie may have involved some guessing here and there around bright red cherry stains dripped by little fingers that left proper measurements up to the imagination.

The family learned to ignore what was lost in favor of what was found; a hundred new memories for every forgotten spell, a proud family lineage listed and remembered each time another generation opened the book. They learned to ignore the stickier pages and grosser stains as much as they all instinctively knew to ignore the signature that they could sometimes see scrawled above the first Rosalie's name in a brighter red than any cherry stain. They ignored the mess in favor of the good, and followed the instructions as they made their own additions to the book; spells, and meals, and name after name after name, signed in the unique cursive of each new family member who committed to the history of their family, each person who focused on the positive instead of how much they could possibly lose.

Everyone knew that it was never just a cookbook. But after so many generations of ignoring, and forgetting, they forgot exactly what it was that they were signing.

Assyrian Machinery

Anne Elise Brinich

Anne Elise Brinich writes and designs
technology.

When I was ten, Tashlutum gave me a granite birdcage with a hinged door, which opened and shut with a soft grinding sound. She was newly queen, and had beautiful crafts within reach at all times, but the birdcage, she told me, was made specially for me. She wanted me to catch laughing doves from the courtyard and put them inside.

"It will be lonely," she said, "without a sister. The doves will be your sisters."

I wondered what I could get Tashlutum that could serve as a replacement for myself. I was no longer confident that, as queen, she was allowed to like the things we both always loved as children: music at mealtimes, limestone carving, story-lamps. Though she was now a goddess and a regent, the most obvious differences in my sister's life, as far as I could tell, were that she ate more fruit, drank more beer, and wore a more pungent pine perfume. And that I saw less of her.

"I'm learning to write," I told her. "I'll write something for you."

"Write something useful," Tashlutum said. She rose from the floor, her handmaidens helping her up.

The two doves I caught came from the courtyard of the temple where I began studying the next day. They were pink and blue—beautiful, gentle things that milled around the cage, chuckling, while I practiced writing with my tutors. I fed them seeds between lessons, studying the carved geometry of the cage, the perfect metal cylinder slotted through the frame and the door to make the hinge.

When I saw my sister next, she had two sons and a newly born daughter. Both of my doves had died; I buried them in the temple crypt, arranging seeds by their nearly weightless bodies. The cage had been empty for four years, but I cleaned and dusted it often, applying oil to the hinge and sketching my own design for improvements.

The queen's daughter, my niece, was two months old. Tashlutum let me hold her: Ninzuana. Tiny and warm, trembling with life, she too smelled of pine. I wanted to wrap myself around her and turn to stone, protecting her soft form.

"She looks like you," I said to Tashlutum.

"Through my eyes, she looks like you," Tashlutum told me. She was sipping a cup of beer, watching me hold her daughter. In Tashlutum's mind, I had remained a child over the passing years, and to see me with a baby in my arms, she told me, was strange. I held Ninzuana, thinking of the birdcage her mother had built for me, thinking of the wonders I could make for her to play with. After a few moments, she began to wail; her mother took her back and gave the rest of her beer to me.

Two years later, Aduanna, the second princess, was born. I was in Erdun, recording the production of flour using a new milling process I had designed. She was a month old before a messenger traveling from the palace told me: Tashlutum was dead. She had been ill after Aduanna was born and died from a fever. Her body was interred in the royal temple's crypt, which I could visit in Ur to pay my respects when my documentation of the new technology was done. The high priest of Ur was interested in my mechanical improvements to the milling process; my recent induction as a priestess meant I was beholden to him.

I did not return to the hanging gardens of the palace ziggurat, nor its crypt, for another three years, when I was invited to design, test, and document mechanical instrumentation there, which had become a genuine fascination of mine in Erdun. After my success creating the water elevators for the wheat fields of Erdun, the high priest had commanded that all priests and priestesses study mechanics. I had been assigned a young acolyte who recorded my research and designs.

When I visited the palace tomb to pay my respects to my sister, I brought a bronze box with me. Her crypt had been sealed; the king, though upset at his wife's death, was done with her. There would be no entering the inside of the little structure around her body, though it had been heaped with flowers at some point after her passing. Brittle brown stems were still stuck in the alleys on the tomb's reliefs.

I thought about leaving the box I'd constructed at her tomb, but curiosity won, as it often did with me—I asked my acolyte to find someone who could introduce me to my nieces.

Ninzuana was six; Aduanna was three. They both played in the gardens during the day. Their brothers, busy with their studies and the relative freedom of being slightly older, no longer found them to be interesting company. I introduced myself to Ninzuana, wondering at how the infant I'd held had turned into a walking, speaking being.

"I brought you a gift," I told her, leading her over to where her sister sat on a handmaiden's lap. She followed, still not certain who I was or what my intentions were. Her dark eyes, her pine scent, Tashlutum leapt from her daughter's face—accusing me of being absent and useless, of failing my nieces.

"What is it?" Ninzuana asked, looking at the bronze box, which I held at the sides. I crouched down so she could look at the etchings, the relief of the mourning doves on the top and bottom.

"You open it," I told her, pushing the top up with my finger so that the lid lifted by its hinge a small bit.

Ninzuana pushed the lid open and the gold bird sprung out, unfolding its wings and uncovering its head from its resting place in its metal plumage. Ninzuana screamed and fell backwards; Aduanna shrieked with delight, and her handmaiden wrapped an arm around Aduanna's body so that she could cover her own laughing mouth with the other hand. My acolyte, behind me, was silent, though she too had jumped as the bird emerged.

"You tricked me," sobbed Ninzuana, from the ground.

"No, no," I assured her. "Look." And despite having no reason to trust me, she looked as I closed the lid of the box slowly, the metal bird folding back into itself, fitting its head back into its chest, then tucking its wings back beside its body.

"Is it real?" Ninzuana wanted to know. She sat back up and cautiously lifted the lid, watching the bird begin to unfold.

"It's not a real bird," I told her. "It's made out of metal."

"But it moves like a real bird," Ninzuana said. She opened the box all the way, peering at the bird and hunching her shoulders as if it were about to fly at her face.

"It's a present for you. And for Aduanna. To play with."

Aduanna had recovered from her laughter and was also looking curiously at the bird in the box, reaching out her hand to touch it.

"She'll break it," Ninzuana told me.

"I'll make another if she breaks it."

"You made this?"

"Yes. Do you like it?"

"I didn't like it at first," Ninzuana admitted. But when I held out the box for her to take, she closed the lid and put it under her arm, using her leg to keep the heavy box steady against her chest. "I like it now, though."

"Share it with your sister," I instructed.

I stayed at the palace for a few months. It would have been better for me to leave, to go back to the farmlands and oversee the creation of the sowing technology, but the high priest asked me to stay and practice with him. He was curious about my mechanical designs; he admitted that, besides himself, the other priests and priestesses showed none of my passion for them. He was an exceptional engineer, and though abrupt in manner and intimidating, he seemed to find kinship in the mechanical nature of the machinery we designed despite seeing a more individual application for them. Together, we rigged the king's Temple of Ninurta with enormous sliding doors; the heads of the lamassu on either sides of the entrance bowed when they were opened.

My sister's husband did not remarry. He was mourning, the high priest told me. Servants and acolytes verified this for me, defying the sealed door of my sister's tomb and the long-wilted flowers. He was disturbed by the swiftness of his wife's death, how powerless he had been as she succumbed. He began to curtail

Ninzuana and Aduanna's time with others, especially if he perceived their companions to be unhealthy; the metrics by which he measured this were clear only to him. With my proximity to the high priest, I was perceived as a beacon of fitness. They were allowed all the time in the world with me, and they began to linger around my workshop after their midday meals, watching my acolyte and me work.

I thought at first that it must be tedious for them, but it was thrilling for me. I would show them the tiny models we made, of thin reeds and wood, meant for larger-scale production of mills powered by the water flowing down farming hills. I let them trickle little streams into the tiny mills, and they pointed out how the system worked to me, from the force of the cogs to the milling wheel that crushed the wheat. I reveled in their interest—it was everything to me that the daughters of my sister could see how knowledge could be applied to create, to improve. They recommended alterations and additions: what else could the mill crush? Grapes? Rocks? Could I make a device like this that they could use in the bath, to spin the water around? Could I make something that made the water stay warm? Could I make something that made more water?

Aduanna's hearing was very bad, and not being able to communicate with the ease of her sister frustrated her. She was not above crushing the models if left alone with them, especially if her sister had been teasing her. I began to let her play with things we were planning to throw out anyway. She would rip the blotched papers apart and crush unusable materials into dust, then look at me, daring me to tell her to stop. She would pound a single rock on the ground of the workshop for half an hour, making a ruckus that drove her sister into teary fits.

She had a fury that had not existed in her mother and that her sister also lacked. When our gazes met, her eyes scrubbed mine, challenging me, as if I were an object whose design was innately imperfect. Perhaps it was a trait from her father, the living deity, who I had never seen.

She drove both the acolyte and her sister away one afternoon with her destruction. I knelt down beside her after I realized she was rubbing her hands raw, scraping stones along the floor of the workshop.

"What are you doing, Aduanna?"

She looked at me and stopped scraping. The brown dust from the stones had turned her arms gray up to her shoulders. "Nothing."

"Are you making something?"

"No," she said. She cracked the rock at the ground.

"Your sister left because of the noise. Do you want to go find her?"

"No."

We stared at each other for a moment. Then, Aduanna lifted a dusty hand and grabbed my nose, twisting.

I swiped her hand away—she lifted her other hand and hit my face with her open palm.

"Aduanna!" I held both of her hands down. She looked shocked at the anger that rose on my face. "Why did you hit me?"

She wouldn't answer, but tears pooled in her eyes. I felt her arms slacken, and I let them go; she sat back onto the floor and cried. Eventually, I left her and went back to my work. She fell asleep on the floor, red-faced, until a handmaid came to look for her.

Was it a stranger's anger that I saw in her face, or my own? I thought of the lamassus' heads that bowed when the king entered his temple. I thought of my sister's tomb, a monument to her fertility.

I left a few weeks later, to the relief of my acolyte. There was a tension between the princesses and I now that I did not want to name. I was not their mother—I had never been like their mother—and they were too young for me to explain that to them. I repaired the mills in Erdun, which broke or rotted easily. I began to work on a design for a lightweight plowing drill. I sent the princesses messages each month illustrating the tools I worked on—it was more correspondence than I had with the high priest, who would have coveted such information.

After four years in Erdun, I received a message from the palace in Ur. The princesses were dead. Their brother had killed a visiting dignitary's son, and the dignitary had requested a sacrifice from the king: his son, or both of his daughters. The two girls had been poisoned after a lavish meal—a painless death, the messenger assured me, and one that their divine father could control, which meant everything to his peace of mind. The high priest was overseeing the construction of their tomb in the palace crypt, which would be as beautiful, if not more, than their mother's. The king had loved them dearly.

I did not pack much, and I did not finish my work in Erdun. I thought of what I would do upon entering the castle, what I would tell the king.

I returned to the palace with the messenger, a sleepless journey of a week, going directly to the crypt late at night. A sandstone structure was being erected directly beside my sister's tomb, larger than my sister's and showing ornate trappings motivated by a guilty father: a pink limestone stele with story carvings of gods and children, seven feet high, and matching reliefs wrapping around the tomb's perimeter like a scroll.

I stepped inside—the tomb was still open, construction ongoing. Torches were lit around the chamber inside, their heat amplifying a ferocious stench. A small trench of water flowed around the dais in the middle of the chamber, which did nothing to condition the scent. On the dais lay the small corpses of Aduanna and Ninzuana, embalmed, bloated, arranged in sleeping positions, thin ropes tied around their limbs. I recognized miniature versions of my latest water mill design in the trench below the dais, lifted so that they were not yet operating.

The high priest and an acolyte were at work inside, and the priest lifted his head as I entered the chamber. It seemed every study, illustration, and manual he had ever glanced at was inside. A library of scrolls and carvings were stacked up on the wall behind him, around a desk where he and the acolyte had constructed the mechanism before me. I recognized in a glance, drawings I had sent to the princesses.

The high priest stowed the paper he and the acolyte had been studying, greeting me warmly. I said nothing—I was certain I would be sick. I did not look at the princesses.

"You have come to mourn them," the high priest surmised. "Their father is also grieving. He asked that we prepare a special presentation for their bodies, and we have indeed. We are hoping that he will be less melancholy when he sees the wonder we've created here." The priest swept his hand toward the girls, but I did not look. A fabrication occurred to me; a lazy, deadly lie.

"It is a machine," the priest told me, somehow interpreting my silence as curiosity. "To reanimate the princesses. To show how they were in life. That is what their father requested we do: show them as they were in life. It is because of mechanics that we are able to do so. Look at this."

He gestured at the acolyte, who adjusted and opened the spout of the cistern near their desk. There was a rush of the water stream into the trenches on the ground, and the priest lowered the mills into the water around the dais.

With the force of the water, the mills began to spin, pulling at levers beneath the dais. The ropes attached to the levers creaked—they began to spin, tugging at the ropes around the corpses' legs, hips, and arms. After a few moments, the corpse of Aduanna sat up, raising an arm at us. I saw the movement, but I could not focus on the body—my eye would not lift to the face of the corpse, they would only see the individual motions of the parts, where the ropes connected to the more mechanical features of its body. Ninzuana's corpse struggled to move— it shifted slightly on the table—one leg came off the dais, then dropped again.

"We are still working on Ninzuana," the acolyte assured me.

"This is the greatest application of mechanics we have yet discovered," the high priest said. "This is what technology is for. What do you say? This is a great honor for your nieces and for you. You have brought them a second life."

I made myself look at the face of the sitting corpse. Gray-blue skin puckered around the nose, mouth and closed eyes. The head was tilted back a little, propped up by a board that ran from the back of Aduanna's head along her spine. Her hand was still lifted in a greeting to us. "This is not life," I said to the priest. "This is use."

He shook his head as Aduanna's head turned towards me. For a moment, I remembered the slap she'd delivered to me after crushing rocks on the floor of my workshop. The corpse's hand lowered slowly to the dais.

I heard the priest mutter beside me, asking the acolyte to lift the mills. The acolyte obeyed, and in the moment both she and the priest were focused on the water trench, Aduanna rose from the dais and took a step towards us, a soft thump sounding as she landed on the ground. She was slow but solid, and much stronger than she had been years ago when I saw her last. The decomposition of her face seemed to amplify the rage I'd seen in it.

The machinery on the dais creaked with strain at this new movement, and the high priest and acolyte looked up from their work. The princess took another step towards them and the level beneath the dais snapped—the ropes holding her left leg went slack. Another snap broke the right leg's restraints.

We were frozen. The corpse approached us, lifeless, rotten eyes observing all three of us at once. The levers on the dais broke one by one, until she was just a footstep in front of us.

"Princess Aduanna, our machinery has given you movement!" The high priest declared. He was shaking. "You are stronger now in your second life. Praise the gods and the king!"

She plunged a hand at his stomach. At first I thought she was only striking him with her fist, not causing much more damage than when she'd slapped me across the face years before. As she withdrew the hand, I saw that she was holding a thin metal rod.

The priest gasped in pain and the acolyte rushed forward, attempting to bat the rod from Aduanna's hands. She sliced at his face, once drawing a red line from his forehead to his mouth, then again, across his neck. She stabbed into the priest's chest, six times, unbottling screams. When the acolyte was silent, she cut the ropes around her sister's body. Then she set the tomb aflame, starting with the designs.

Even when I ran out of the tomb, yelling for help, it took a few moments for anyone to come to my aid. Smoke was billowing out of the entrance, smothering the stars in the night sky. Soot covered my hands and feet and I stumbled across the courtyard to the wall of the ziggurat, coughing. Eventually, people came, drawn to the smoke and the cracking sound of flames. The ceiling began to cave in as I was drawn away by guards.

This is what I told the king, a few hours later, when I found myself in his presence. I had never seen him before, and I was relieved that there was nothing familiar about him. He shook his head after I told him of the abuse of his daughters' remains.

"It is true, I told the High Priest to show them as they were in life," the king said. His voice was deep but dry, like an empty well. "But my power disturbed the gods, as it always does. They are not ready for one more powerful than them."

I was shaking. Smoke and my bitter perspiration had soaked into my clothes; I was aware how unimpressive I looked, how lost. It dawned on me that he did not doubt any part of my story; that to him, it was reasonable his daughters would return from the dead. It was a testament to his power, that he might make the dead return to life.

And a second realization: that everything I had ever made, had made his belief in his own power grow.

"You look so much like my wife Tashlutum." The king gestured at me. "You will stay here, and bathe. You are grieving, like me." He rose and approached me, jewels rustling as he stood. When he was close to me, he lifted my chin to look at him.

"My poor girls," he said. "I wanted them to live."

I dug the rod out of my sleeve. I stabbed him, too, sinking the weapon into his soft belly, then ripping it out, and sending it into his throat.

Giant Beach

Amy E. Porter

Amy is a writer who lives, works, and
reads in Annapolis, Maryland.

There is a place near the sea where they say the light behaves strangely, where the words you speak echo back to you across the waves, saying something else entirely. Here, too, the pieces of far-off, crumbling giants have come ashore and are melting slowly in the sun while the relentless, northern waves wash over them.

On the shores of Iceland, the clouds toss the sun between them like a ball, high in the frigid air, and the black sand exorcises shadow and absorbs demons from all who visit there. A cleansing place.

I went when they said a whole eye had been beached there. The most complete piece they'd had in years, they said. I watched the footage online of it coming in with the tide. It bobbed closer, then ebbed away, until, finally, after hours of slowly drifting nearer and nearer, it all at once landed with a mighty splash. I stopped the video and watched it again.

After weeks of nothing in my life mattering, suddenly something did. I had to go see it. This was a once in a lifetime opportunity, and I didn't have long left to live.

I hadn't known what to say to my doctor when he told me my body was dying. I felt fine, just a little tired, shaky. I thought it was nerves at starting the new job, or maybe sleep deprivation (I'd always had restless nights).

It wasn't either of those.

ALS, amyotrophic lateral sclerosis, and three years on average to live, if you called being forced to experience the slow breakdown of every muscle in your body living. I wished with all my heart that I had something that would kill me faster.

"What should I do?" I asked him.

He shook his head sadly at me. "Get some specialists on board, keep trying treatments. There are things we can do to make it easier and to slow your body's deterioration. Ultimately, you have to prepare yourself and your loved ones. You'll be tempted to shut them out. My best advice is: Don't." He awkwardly patted me on the back as I was leaving his office, "I'm sorry. It's unfair, it really is."

I knew it was. It was unfair. As anyone would say who heard my story, my death signified nothing other than waste. What could I accomplish in three years? With my body set to fail at every turn, I had no potency anymore. I had never felt so insignificant.

I didn't take my doctor's advice, either. I felt I needed to be alone. I couldn't face seeing my family and friends, or them seeing me. The time limit I'd been set brutally reminded me how much I had depended on having years of my life left to fix all the relationships I'd broken. I scrolled through my friends on social media and knew that every one of them had reason to be angry with me. What would happen if I told them I was dying?

I disconnected all of my accounts and turned off my phone.

I spent my days in the welcome distraction of engaging in

obscure research. I found an article in a science magazine about the discovery of giants in the arctic circle. Frozen for who knows how long inside massive mountains of ice, we were completely unaware of them until the glaciers, icebergs, and ice shelves started cracking and liquefying. Then, with more and more frequency over the past couple years, pieces of colossi washed up on beaches all over the northern hemisphere, and especially in Iceland. Paleontologists believe that this was the gigantic race's home.

I scrolled through the different drawings of what a whole giant would have been like. Humanoid, but shaggy like Bigfoot, and with a strange, jellyfish like transparency to their skin and bones. Cave dwellers, perhaps, or maybe creatures exclusively belonging to an ice age, designed to blend in against the blinding white reflection of sun-on-snow.

I wondered how long it took for them to become extinct. As climate change reshaped their environment, they would have struggled to adapt, and eventually, inevitably, they failed to. I wondered if they knew that they would fail, that natural selection would pass them by.

When the video of the eye showed up on a live feed, I bought my plane ticket. I also purchased a cane. My walking was getting shakier, and I wanted to ensure that I could stand and study this natural wonder for as long as I wanted. Alone.

This one trip made up my whole bucket list, a thing I never thought I'd need until now. *Before I die, I'd like to see this one thing in person* was a thought process that had never taken place in my head before. Yet, as I flew through the clouds, I found myself thinking of the trip as a final pilgrimage.

There was something about that eye. Maybe it was just the bevy of images I'd already gone through, where all that had surfaced on the beach were broken fragments, in contrast to the eye's whole being, or maybe it was the idea of something so personal, so distinct to life as an eye. Either way, I felt compelled.

***

Like every shore I'd ever been to, that beach in Iceland felt like coming to the edge of the world. I looked out across the shadowy sands, facing into the wailing wind coming from where the gray sea met the paler gray sky, and I thought that this edge must face towards death.

I was alone on that particular day, no tourists. It had just stormed, and the water was high, sloshing large waves with full bellies onto the shore, where they burst, spraying me with their freezing innards. In amongst them, and littering the shoreline, I saw various shattered body parts: a severed thumb, its icy tendons spiking out of one end, the coiled chunk of a brain, a giant rib. The smallest of these was the size of a car. Their contours were blurred, and I could see how pitted their surfaces had become. In a few more days, they'd be unrecognizable. I hurried past them, as fast as I could hobble while digging my cane into the sand, to find the object of my interest.

The eye had been flung a couple hundred yards away from where the rest of the remains lay. The waves sucked at the very bottom of it, where it was partly sunken into the ground. With an axis the height of a man, from far away, it looked like a huge, foggy blue marble had rolled out of the sea. But the closer I got to it, the more excited I grew, until, when I was actually standing in front of it, and it had devoured my vision, I laughed louder than I had in weeks. It was perfect. The sleek, wet retina arched above me in unbroken roundness. As I looked at it, the sun soared between two clouds and its rays shot through the transparent eyeball and filled it with warmth for the moment. I was almost blinded. It was more light than the light itself, and it glimmered out over the shadowy sand like bomb shrapnel. When my own eyes recovered, as if it were an all-encompassing crystal, I gazed into its depths. The sun's rays bounced joyously off of every retinal vein, but I saw past them into the lens and through the pupil on the other side.

Back towards me, over the seal-smooth backs of the waves, came the echoes of my laughter, now sounding hysterical, like someone in an ecstasy of grief.

I looked through the eye. All around was black, spherical space. Spherical because it encircled, it never turned a corner or split a seam. The blackness was everything there was. Like a sudden burst of choral music, the sun bloomed into being. Behind it, the stars' tiny, silver lanterns swayed far away in a distant wind. Our Earth was there, too. And in the time it takes to read a sentence, I watched it blossom into seas and into flowers. The eye saw every glorious mountain range, every dinosaur, and it saw every grain of sand and every fruit fly. I saw them too, all at the same time. I couldn't comprehend it, but I saw. It took only a few moments for life to swarm my senses.

It was too much. I staggered back, barely catching myself with my cane. I struggled to get my breath.

"Good God," I said, "glorious."

Good, said God. Remember how glorious, whispered the sea.

The sun was being caught by the next cloud, soon its rays would vanish. I squinted at the sky. I had to look, one more time.

I actually placed my hand on its huge surface as I bent forward to look again.

The waves were sloshing at my feet. My toes were far past being numb, and I could feel my limbs shaking at the effort of holding me upright.

It was all dark, again. The stars burned fainter, as if they had picked up their lanterns and carried them farther away. The sun rolled lazily over the horizon. It looked bloated. Under its light, I saw nothing but a dust cloud, tossing like a restless sleeper. No more blooming, no more life, just scarred and bitter desolation was present on the earth. The scene before me appeared to howl.

The sun went in, and the eye was no longer transparent, but foggy again. Under my palm, the surface moistened, sending small rivulets down my arm. I stepped back from the eye. Where my hand had pressed it, a small dent interrupted its roundness.

The tide was coming in. The water now reached above my ankles. If I didn't leave soon, I might not be able to walk.

Nevertheless, I forced myself to journey around the rim, through the incoming tide, leaning painfully on my cane, until I was standing in front of the iris. Webbing out from the hollow pupil was a perfect circle of color on the larger sphere, and that color was untouched, oceanic blue.

I knew it was looking at me. It might once have seen which dust particles I would make up in that post-apocalyptic sandstorm. The pupil widened, inviting me in once again. I yielded to it, bending forward, the eye and me face-to-face. In it, I could see my own reflection, and in that single image, I saw every reflection of myself I'd ever glimpsed. Only my face seemed softened, as if by love or memory. The waves continued to pass to and from us, and, as I looked out again into the tide, it seemed as though the eye gave birth to the ocean. As if it cried the briny spray into being.

I no longer thought about walking away, I didn't think I could have even if I'd wanted. I was so cold that my whole body was bound stiff and tight with it. I barely felt it when my legs gave out and I collapsed into the rising water. I leaned against the eye, as if it had been a friend's shoulder, and let my cane wash away with the black sand.

"Perhaps," I murmured, "a few of those tears are for me."

The sea blew back no answer but a sigh.

Halfway Through the Dark

Alexis Ames

Alexis Ames is a writer living in Colorado who first picked up a pen when she was eleven years old and hasn't put it down since. Science fiction is her preferred genre–more specifically, exploring the changing relationship between humans and technology. Her work has previously appeared in publications such as Pseudopod, Kyanite Press, and The New Accelerator. She can be found on Twitter at @alexis_writes1, and a list of her current and upcoming stories can be found on her blog at alexisames.home.blog.

She hadn't intended for the man to die.

Granted, he *had* done his best to kill her. Unfortunately, now he was leaking blood and brain matter onto her grandmother's rug, and she would never hear the end of it once her mother found out.

But there was no time to worry about that now.

"Beverly!" she called. She lifted her skirts and stepped over the man's body, pistol tucked back in the holster slung around her waist. "Edgar!"

Silence. The house was lit from ground floor to attic, nearly every lamp ablaze, but no one answered her calls. The door to Beverly's lab stood ajar, and the cavernous room beyond was silent. A roaring fire had been built in the grate in the library, but it had been left untended.

The house was empty.

Unease curdling her gut, Kate picked up the telephone receiver and had the switchboard connect her to the station.

"Sergeant Hawkins," a voice answered crisply.

"David," she said tightly, "they're gone."

"Who?" he demanded, but she heard the thread of alarm in his voice.

"I need you here," she said. "Immediately."

***

He arrived alone less than an hour later, still in his uniform, truncheon on one hip and pistol on the other. Kate met him at the door.

"When did you notice them gone?" he asked. Water beaded on his shoulders and dripped from his dark hair. Sometime in the past hour, it had started to rain.

"I called you right away." Kate hesitated. "Well...I killed a man, first."

David gave her a weary look, but gestured for her to lead the way.

Upstairs, in the study, he knelt a careful six inches away from the body. He peered at the dead man's face and said, "I don't know him."

"Do you know *everyone* in Chicago?"

Fear made her snappish; the words came out sharp. David pushed himself to his feet and gave her a look.

"I know the faces of the men who want you dead, yes," he said. "He isn't one of them."

"That you know of," Kate countered. "That list seems to grow by the day."

David rubbed his forehead. The perpetual smudges under his eyes seemed darker than usual today, and his face was drawn.

"Hell," he muttered. "What a day."

Despite herself, Kate felt a prickling curiosity down her spine. She hadn't worked a case for David—and, by extension, the police—in almost a month. In this city, that was downright unusual. "Something I should know about?"

"Nothing you can help with. Murder victim went missing this morning. Shot dead in the middle of the night, no witnesses, and now the body's gone. The chief will have someone's head for it, probably mine." David sighed. "Are you certain they were home?"

Kate nodded. "Beverly had lectures all morning at the university and would have been home by noon. Edgar was here, recharging. It takes him nearly a full day to recharge, and we were working all night.'"

David lifted an eyebrow at her. "Something *I* should know about?"

"Flu took an entire family in twenty-four hours." She shook her head. "We had to prepare the bodies, that's all."

"I assume you sent word to the morgue about him." David nudged the dead man with his boot.

"No, there's no time." She drew a breath. "We're doing this here."

David went pale under his beard, but nodded tightly.

"What do you need me to do?"

"Hold him still."

After a moment's hesitation, David knelt over the body. He

pinned the man's legs together with his knees and then leaned his full weight on the man's arms, holding the body down. It wasn't perfect, but it would have to do.

"Be prepared," Kate said.

"For what?"

"He might thrash a bit."

David stared at her. She lifted one shoulder in a shrug. He had never seen her work in the morgue, only benefited from the results of it. She watched the muscles in his jaw tense as he steeled himself.

"I can handle it," he said. "Do what you need to do."

Whether he could or not was immaterial; he was going to have to deal with whatever happened, because she had no other options and *someone* had taken her only assistant.

"You're going to feel strange," she said. She knelt by the man's head and placed one hand on what was left of his forehead. "Electrified. Try to ignore it."

And then she closed her eyes, shutting out David and any response he might have given. She focused all of her senses inward, reached into the darkness—

—and *pulled.*

The skin under her hand quickly grew warm, and then hot. She pulled harder, reaching through the void, until she saw the tiniest speck of light. She reached for it, reached for it, *reached for it*—

Starbursts exploded around her, illuminating the void, spider webs of flame filling her vision. Voices came to her, fragments of conversations she had never witnessed, all of them male and unfamiliar.

Be quiet—

—shut down the mech-

They're downstairs—

Tie her up!

A burst of images came out of the fire, flickering and half-formed, shadows dancing across a canvas. She caught impressions of— *buildings electric lamps a park full of green grass fire a castle pistols*—but soon as she grasped for one to hold on to, to examine, it slipped away from her. Her hand burned. The fire chased her. The closer she got to an image, the hotter it burned. She smelled cooking meat—

—and found herself gasping on the floor of the study, David's worried face filling her vision. He was as white as her petticoat, and his grip on her upper arms bordered on painful. She would have bruises there in the morning.

"I didn't know what was happening," he said in a rush. "The body—it was moving. Thrashing, like you said, but then your hand—it looked like it was burning. I had to shove you away to break the connection, I'm sorry, I didn't know what else to do."

She turned over her left hand, gazing blankly at the blistering palm. She hadn't had a mishap like this in years; Edgar made sure of it. She got to her feet and went over to her desk, pulling out salve and bandages that she kept in the top drawer. She smeared the burn cream on her hand and wrapped it hastily. It would have to do for now.

"Did you get what you needed?" David asked.

"There was so much damage to his brain." She grimaced at the body. Why couldn't she have shot him somewhere else, like the gut or the heart? She would have been able to gather a clearer vision of the final minutes of his life then. She pushed the thought aside—lingering over regrets wasted crucial minutes. "I was only able to get impressions. He seemed to feel strongest about a park, and—a castle?"

David blinked at her, and then she saw recognition light his eyes. "The museum."

The Palace of Fine Arts, from the Exposition—now the Field Columbian Museum. Of course. She'd passed the grand building dozens of times in her life. When set against the backdrop of the grimy city and the miserable, gray lake, it seemed woefully out of place.

"That must be where they are," she said. It was as good a place to start as any; she had no idea where else to begin.

David's gaze drifted away from her, fixing on a spot over her left shoulder. She turned, eyes sweeping the bookcases from ceiling to floor, but she didn't see what had caught his attention until he was halfway across the room.

A handful of gears and wires lay on the floor, scattered as though someone had tossed them carelessly aside. David crouched, reaching out a hand—but he stopped short of touching the gears, fingers hovering less than an inch above them.

"He fought," David said quietly after a moment.

Of course he would have. Edgar would have fought to the last to protect Beverly.

David got to his feet again, his eyes hard when he looked at Kate.

"We're going to get them back."

***

David hailed a carriage on the street outside while Kate reloaded her pistol and grabbed a couple of knives for insurance. She strapped them to her wrists, and pulled down her sleeves to cover them. She had no idea what kind of resistance to expect or even who was behind this, but one thing was certain—they had taken her wife, and she intended to have Beverly back by dawn.

"What do you think we're walking into?" David asked, once the carriage door was shut and the driver had spurred the horses on.

"I wish I knew," Kate said. "These might not even be my enemies. Beverly's a renowned engineer—"

"And you're the one who can speak to the dead."

"I *don't* speak to the dead," Kate corrected swiftly. "I can only see their final few minutes of life, *if* the body is fresh, *if* the brain is intact. My abilities are incredibly limited. They're not useful to anyone outside of your line of work."

"Your abilities are incredibly misunderstood," David countered. "To some, they might sound like a shot at immortality, and some people *would* kill for that."

He hardly needed to remind *her* of that. She understood that better than anyone, which he well knew. Stung, she turned to the window, watching the black night speed by.

"You should have told him."

Beside her, David stiffened. With forced nonchalance, he said blandly, "I don't know what you're talking—"

"Edgar." She turned back to him, pinning him in place with her glare. "You should have told him how you feel. Now, it might be too late."

"Don't talk about what you don't understand," David said fiercely.

"Then neither should you."

They passed the rest of the journey in silence.

***

Palace was an apt name for the building that dominated the park. It was a looming, intimidating structure, and seemed like the perfect way to call unwanted attention to oneself.

But then, perhaps that had been the intent.

David broke into the building with practiced ease, which Kate would have teased him about on any other night. But not here, not tonight. Not when Beverly's life depended on everything going perfectly, on them not making a single misstep.

Kate hadn't been inside this building since the Exposition, and she'd been a child then. In the intervening years, it had been transformed from a gallery to a museum, and that coupled with the darkness meant she was as unfamiliar with it as if she had never before stepped foot inside of it.

David, however, crossed the floor with ease. She hurried to stay in his wake, following the sound of his muffled footfalls, so as not to bump into any unexpected exhibits. A moment later, light flared, and she reeled back from it. But it was only a lantern, held aloft by David.

"You've been here before," she said quietly, almost an accusation.

David nodded, his face made eerie by yellow lamplight. "If I hadn't joined the police, I might have—"

He broke off, shaking his head. "Where do you think they could be?"

"You know this place better than I do." Kate turned in a circle. They stood in a cavernous hall, and a shudder crawled down her spine as she took in the faint outlines of a massive skeleton, and a beast she never would have been able to dream up, not even in her wildest dreams. "What is *that?*"

"A mastodon," David answered, and then he shook his head. "This is too exposed, they wouldn't be here. They'd want a room that offered them a tactical advantage. Somewhere we couldn't take them by surprise. Come on, upstairs."

Kate couldn't see most of the exhibits they passed on their way through the great hall and up the wide stone steps, and thought that was likely for the best. When they reached the top of the steps, David extinguished the lamp, and she looked at him askance. But then her gaze was drawn by a sliver of light at the end of the corridor, which she hadn't seen with the lantern lit.

She felt David reach for his pistol, and put a hand on his arm.

"They're expecting us," she said in an undertone.

"All the more reason for us to be ready for them," David said quietly. "The dead are your realm. Living criminals are mine."

"But they're expecting *me*, and I'm no use to them dead. They won't hurt me." She moved slightly ahead of him in the corridor. "Follow me."

He sighed, but acquiesced, hand falling away from his hip and pistol left in place. She still kept as quiet as possible as she moved down the corridor, but her skirts rustled and her boots clicked against the stone floors, and there was no way they could have masked their approach even if they'd wanted to.

The door at the end of the hall was open, and the steady light told Kate that the room inside had been lit by electric lamps. She stepped into the open doorway.

"Ah, Dr. Brooks. Or should I say detective? You're early."

In the center of the room stood a table with what was clearly a body on it—it had been covered with a white sheet, but the shape was unmistakable. Edgar was nearby, his photoreceptors dark, seemingly powered down. His carapace gaped open, revealing the wires and gears in his chest cavity. And then there was Beverly, her arms bound behind her back, standing there with shackles around her ankles.

"Sorry, Katie," she said, her mouth twisting with regret. Kate shook her head.

"Doctor is fine," she told the man, who stood near Edgar with his hands clasped behind his back. "What do you want?"

"Interesting piece of technology, this mech man of yours." The man laid a hand on Edgar's metal shoulder. The mech didn't move. "He's your assistant, yes?"

"You already know the answer to that."

The man snorted, amused. "Indeed. You could do so much more with him, you know. Combined with your abilities, the two of you make quite an invaluable team."

"We're already a team."

"You're a coroner and he's your assistant. A damn waste, if you ask me, but that's none of my concern at the moment. You can speak to the dead, and you're going to help me."

"You kidnapped her wife and her assistant, and left a man behind in her house to kill her." David took a step forward, so he stood shoulder-to-shoulder with Kate. "She's not going to do a damn thing for you."

The man bared his teeth in a grin. "She took my bait, as I thought she would. She killed the man I left behind and spoke to him in the beyond. That's how she knew where to find us. Or am I wrong, Doctor?"

Kate felt her hands curl into fists, and forced her fingers to relax. Her knees felt weak, and she worried for a moment that her legs might not be able to support her weight. Stupid, *stupid*. She'd fallen right into his trap.

"I thought not. I'm Aldous Cantrell, by the way. It's a pleasure to finally meet you."

Cantrell. She knew that name. She glanced at Beverly, who gave her a regretful look. *Of course.*

"You work at the university, too," she said. And he must be on loan to the museum in some capacity—curator of one of the collections, most likely.

"It's how I was able to gain access to your house this evening." Cantrell gave a thin smile. "Your wife thought I was there to discuss business. And as fascinating as this has all been, we're wasting time."

He drew back the sheet on the table, and David sucked in a breath.

"Your missing victim, I assume," Kate said to him without taking her eyes off Cantrell, and he nodded.

"My son," Cantrell said, and Kate closed her eyes. "Shot dead in the street last night, slain like an *animal*. You're going to bring him back."

"I can't," Kate said. "I can only—"

"*Lies!*" Cantrell hissed. He pulled out a pistol and pressed it to the side of Beverly's head. "You would bring her back, if I shot her."

"If you kill Beverly, you're never getting her help," David said vehemently.

"I believe she can speak for herself," Cantrell said. He looked at Kate. "Well?"

"No." Kate's mouth was too dry to swallow. "No, I wouldn't bring her back, because I can't. No more than I can bring back your son. I can't even access his final memories. The body has been dead for too many hours. I'm sorry."

Cantrell's mouth twisted.

"That's how little she thinks of you, her *wife*," he snarled at Beverly. "She won't even come to your aid when you need her the most. Does she also have so little regard, I wonder, for the one she rescued from a scrap heap all those years ago?"

He plunged his left hand into Edgar's chest cavity and *pulled*. Out came a handful of wires, gears, tiny electrical bulbs, and Edgar opened his mouth and screamed. The sound was ear-splitting, like a thousand tiny ice-pricks inside her ears, and Kate recoiled.

David lunged forward. Faster than a blink, Cantrell's arm went up and the pistol went off. In the confined space of the room, the *crack* was deafening, and Kate's eyes were dazzled by the afterimage of the flash of the shot. David grunted, staggering back several steps. He gripped his shoulder; when he pulled his hand away, it was soaked in red.

"Another step, and the next bullet goes through his head," Cantrell said quietly. "There's no reason to make this difficult, Doctor."

Kate held up her hands. Her heart pounded like it was trying to escape her ribcage, and sweat trickled between her shoulder blades.

"All right," she said quietly. "Yes, I'll help you. But I'll need Edgar—"

Cantrell ripped out another handful of Edgar's inner parts, and the mech man's scream skittered up the register. Kate clamped her hands over her ears. David let out a pitiful moan.

When it stopped, Cantrell said, "Do you think I'm an idiot? You do this alone, Doctor."

"I can't do this without an assistant." Her ears rang uncomfortably, most of her hearing blotted out. "You'll help me, then."

"Katie, don't," David hissed.

She approached the body. Cantrell's son had been a young man, barely into his twenties. Two bullets to the heart had killed him; if the body hadn't been stolen by his father, he might have ended up on her table today instead.

"I need to touch him," she said, and Cantrell gave a tight nod. He still held the pistol, this time pointed at her. "As my assistant, so will you. You're my conduit. You'll help facilitate the bridge between us, so that I can reach him and bring him—back into this world. Understood?"

He nodded. She gestured for him to lay a hand on his son's fore-head, and then she covered it with her own.

"Ready?" she asked, and before he could answer, she shut her eyes and dove into the abyss, dragging him down with her.

Diving into the mind of someone who had been dead this long was like plunging into an icy lake. Cold filled her veins, and the darkness was a physical presence. There was no light here, no sputtering life, no afterimages from the recently dead. She was immersed in utter *nothingness*. The silence was overwhelming.

Her heart thudded inside her chest; blood pumped through her veins, a steady *thud thud thud*. She could sense that much, even if she couldn't hear it. Her lungs expanded, contracted. Time was meaningless here. It could be minutes, it could be hours.

And then—out of the darkness, a second heartbeat joined hers. She felt it beat in tandem with her own, steady and calm, not at all like the jack-rabbit quick of panic. The cold was bone-deep, like she'd taken a December plunge into Lake Michigan, and her lungs stuttered, losing their rhythm. Her breathing became shallow, quick. Then her heart fell out of sync with the other's, and she knew she didn't have long.

Too quickly, the other presence vanished. Winked out, like a light. She was abruptly alone, adrift, her senses cut off—and if David didn't get to her soon enough—

Kate gasped, dragging in a lungful of cool night air as her eyes flew open. She staggered; David caught her with an arm around her waist, grunting as she fell against him. The room swam into view around her, went fuzzy, and then abruptly crystallized.

"Are you injured?" he asked in a thin voice.

"No," she gasped, drawing grateful lungfuls of air. "I'm fine."

She looked at the body. Cantrell was slumped over it, his head resting on his son's chest, face slack. His eyes were still open, and they darted periodically, as though he was looking at something.

"He's not—dead," David said awkwardly.

"He's as good as," Kate said grimly. She pushed herself upright, and he let go. "He's lost in the void. His body will die from starvation or dehydration, whichever comes first. Even if someone separates the two of them, there's no bringing him back."

"That was foolish," Beverly said as Kate came over to her. She produced a knife from under sleeves and cut the ropes that bound her at the wrists and ankles. "You could have been trapped yourself—"

Kate kissed her. Beverly's hands went to her hips, pulling her in. She tasted incongruously of apples.

When they broke apart, Kate turned her attention to Edgar, and found that David had beaten her to the mech man. He was still bleeding profusely from his shoulder, blood soaking his uniform almost down to his waist, but he didn't seem to notice it. He had a hand on Edgar's carapace.

"Can you fix him?" The question was tentative, as though David didn't truly want to hear the answer.

"What did Cantrell do to him?" Kate stooped to pick up the discarded parts of Edgar's innards.

"Tortured him," Beverly said bitterly. "Thought he could find the answers to your—abilities hidden inside him. When he found nothing, he kidnapped us both and left that man behind for you to find and—kill."

Beverly took the parts from Kate and examined them.

"It'll take some time. Maybe a few days, maybe a few weeks." She sighed. "But I think I can fix him, yes."

David laid a hand on the side of Edgar's face, stroking his thumb across the smooth metal.

"Please do," he said quietly. "There's something I need to tell him."

Beverly raised her eyebrows at Kate, who shook her head in the way that said I'll explain later.

"Come on." Kate took David's uninjured arm. "Life-threatening or not, we need to get you to the hospital. Beverly will take good care of Edgar. We should also probably alert your people that their missing body has been located. Oh, and that there's a dead man at my house."

"Never a dull day with you, Katie, is it," David said wearily, allowing her to pull his arm around her shoulders.

"I like to keep life interesting

The Lotus Wife

Avra Margariti

Avra Margariti is a queer speculative
author. Her work has appeared in Flash
Fiction Online, Lackington's, Vastarien,
and other venues.

She came to life beneath the river mud, enveloped in her mother's earthy womb. The refracted radiance of the sun beckoned to her, so she stretched upward until she emerged through the water's surface.

He was an orphan of no more than fourteen summers, rolled-up pants riddled with holes and fingers scarred from barbed hooks and catfish spines. He was fishing for carp in the riffles, the saw-grass on either side of the river buzzing with insects, when he beheld her: a blush-pink lotus bud growing from the dark mossy river bed.

He did what any wonder-starved orphan does with beautiful things: he plucked the lotus, broke the twining roots, and cradled the blossom in his palms. A cry burst forth from his lips when the bud opened. He dropped the flower, which transformed into a naked girl before his bewildered eyes.

The girl looked about his age, with strawberry blond hair and a flush beneath her smooth brown skin. She was dainty like a teacup and pretty like a kingfisher. The young fisherman and the lotus girl gazed at each other, young love taking root in their hearts.

The orphan boy lived out of his rowboat. When night fell, he covered himself in a dry tarp and reclined against the weathered wood as the lotus girl swam unhurried circles around his anchored boat. He'd dressed her in his spare clothes, and the faded rags trailed behind her in the glassy water like a comet's tail. Entranced, the fisherman moved to the bow of his boat to watch her better. Both reached for the other at the same time, and their fingertips connected. Their eyes widened as they felt each other's pulse flutter beneath the skin like moth wings.

He told her stories, about his travels downstream and about what lay beyond the river. Her eyes shone with newfound wanderlust, and her dusky pink lips uttered three words: "Take me there."

The young fisherman swiftly began the preparations, gathering food, tools and anything else he could scavenge for their new life together. That same night, the eloping couple drifted down the river in the fisherman's rowboat, carried by a stream of guileless dreams.

They moved into a cozy thatched hut with whitewashed walls and a little herb garden. He lied about his age and found a job at the fish plant, a looming slate-gray factory that belched out putrid smoke into the sky. The plant exported packaged fish to foreign lands and seas neither the orphaned fisherman nor the lotus girl had ever visited.

She waited for him each afternoon, curled in the window-seat that looked out onto the dusty road. They called each other husband and wife, muffling shy giggles behind their palms as they cherished every minute in each other's company.

Yet instead of blossoming, the lotus girl slowly withered away. She drew a bath every day, sprinkled rose water in her hair, and dipped her toes into puddles of rainwater, but nothing helped. The air was hard to breathe. The blue of the sky was swallowed by a thick veil of smog. Even the rain felt sharp and smoldering against her skin. As time continued to pass, her dreams became aquatic, filled with the memory of moss-rich mud and crystalline waters.

"What do you long for?" the fisherman asked her on the day that marked a year since their first meeting. Lately, she was too exhausted to leave the house, or even step away from her window. He knelt like a supplicant at her feet, waiting for a revelation. "I can tell you're unhappy. I'll work more shifts. I'll buy you perfumes, colorful saris, and jewelry of silver, gold, and precious stones. You'll look lovelier than all the girls in all the fashion magazines."

The lotus wife looked at her husband with doleful eyes and placed a hand on his cheek. The adolescent peach-fuzz tickled her palm, and her throat constricted with tears.

"I don't want jewelry, fine fabrics, or expensive perfume. I don't dream of seeing my face on a Western magazine cover. It is the mud and the water that I need. My mother, the earth and my father, the river."

Salt water beaded at the corners of the fisherman's eyes, for he could see now that his affection for her had blinded him. His heart felt tender like a fresh bruise as he noticed the way her hair had lost its strawberry sheen, her eyes had been stripped of their world-wonder. The pallor of her skin brought to mind a wax figurine.

Deep in the night, he roused her from sleep and wrapped a crocheted blanket around her shoulders. She could barely walk, so he picked her up and carried her in his arms down the winding dirt road, past smoke-stained houses and wilting flower gardens. She weighed almost nothing. He walked unceasingly until they reached the riverbend, and he removed the palm tree fronds covering his flimsy rowboat. It looked like a walnut-shell cradle, and she a frail figure crumpled inside it, small as a thimble, her color fading away.

He rowed and rowed up the river until his arms burned and the oars chafed his palms. At last, they reached their old village where their fates had first entwined.

The deep, dark blue firmament was clear of smoke here, strewn with myriads of stars. Cicadas chirred in the long grass, an ever-rising crescendo. The orphaned fisherman filled his lungs with the brisk nocturnal air before kneeling by the lotus girl's side.

"Wake up, flower," he whispered against her veined papery lips.

Her eyelids trembled, then fully opened. He placed one last kiss upon her brow before mooring his rowboat and wading to the shallows with her in his arms. Dewey lotus flowers freckled the moonlit surface. He was careful not to disturb them. When he was up to his waist in water, he gently laid her down in the river, their nightclothes soggy and heavy.

"I'm sorry," the young fisherman said. "I should never have taken you away from your home and family."

The lotus girl smiled when the looking-glass water soaked her billowing hair. "It's not your fault. I was willing. I'm in *love*."

"As am I. Which is why I have to let you go."

They held hands as she sank into the silty mud, returning to her mother's wet, dark embrace. By the time dawn broke pink and humid over the mango trees, she was gone from his sight. The fisherman collapsed on the bench seat of his boat and looked down at his trembling hands. Rivulets of mud trickled between his fingers. However, when he unfurled his fists, he saw it: a lock of strawberry blond hair that morphed into a blushing lotus petal before turning into a silvery whispered promise.

To meet again, in this very spot, when both of them had reached full bloom.

THANK YOU TO OUR SUPPORTERS

Many thanks to our patrons and supporters, especially:

Anna O'Brien • Cathrin Hagey • Kathryn Parsons
Amber • Natalie Weizenbaum • Johanna Levene

Aidan Long • Anna Evans • Bonnie Warford
D.M. Domosea • Erik DeBill • Felicia O'Sullivan
Frederick Stark • J'nae Spano • Katie Conrad
Kennon Hulett • Martin Cohen • Mollie Morgeson
Salomao Becker • Sarah Jackson
Tory Hoke • Steven • carol shoemake

Ally Shaw • BethOfAus • Brit Hvide • Carly Racklin
Charlotte Nash-Stewart • Dirck de Lint • Emily Anderson
GriffinFire • J. Askew • Jen G • Jocelyn Actual
Karen Anderson • Kristina Saccone • Leslie Anderson
Maria Haskins • Matthew Bennardo • Rochelle B • Sian Jones
Suzanne Thackston • Wanda • Kayla • willowcabins

Want to see your name here? Become a patron!
patreon.com/lunastation

About the Cover Artist

Christina Kraus is an freelance Illustrator from Germany who enjoys fantasy illustration (and concept art), but is able to work in various other fields aswell. After she got her Bachelor of Arts degree at Hochschule Trier in August 2016 she started, among others, to work for Ulisses Spiele Gmbh (biggest european p&p RPG publisher and distributor) and paints for DSA (The dark eye) and DSK (Die schwarze Katze). She also painted various book covers for self publishers and helped realise crowdfunding projects. Currently she is also working for Humblewood.

Besides drawing and painting Christina likes to spend her time with her friends and family, loves TV-Series like Game of Thrones and Stranger Things, books, nature and animals. Her favourite videogame is Dragon Age: Inquisition.

You can find more of her work at:

www.christinakraus-art.com

NOW AVAILABLE!

THE BEST OF
LUNA STATION QUARTERLY
THE FIRST FIVE YEARS

Featuring fifty stories by emerging women writers,

with cover art by Hugo award-winner Julie Dillon

Luna Station Press is proud to celebrate the fifth anniversary of our flagship Quarterly with this special anthology.

The writers gathered in these pages, from every corner of the globe, are explorers of wonder, magic, and places beyond the stars. They are also explorers of what makes us human, in heart, mind, and spirit.

Come explore the best we have to offer, as we look back fondly on the last five year and look ahead at what's to come.

LUNA STATION PRESS

HELP US GROW,
SUPPORT WOMEN
AUTHORS, AND BRING
GREAT STORIES TO
THE UNIVERSE!

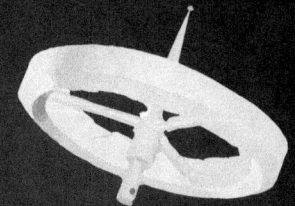

Join the crew of

Luna Station!

BECOME A PATRON AND GRAB YOUR PLACE!

PATREON.COM/LUNASTATION

Want other ways to help?

BUY AN ISSUE OR HELP SPREAD THE WORD ABOUT LSQ
AND THE WONDERFUL WOMEN WRITERS THAT MAKE UP
OUR VIBRANT, CREATIVE COMMUNITY!

Find out more:
LUNASTATIONQUARTERLY.COM

www.ingramcontent.com/pod-product-compliance
Lightning Source LLC
Chambersburg PA
CBHW051511170626
46811CB00002B/766